CLINT

THE BROTHERS OF HASTINGS RANCH SERIES
BOOK SIX

By Katharine E. Hamilton

ISBN-13: 978-1-7358125-8-8

Clint

www.katharinehamilton.com

Cover Design by Kerry Prater.

This is a work of fiction. Names, characters, places,
and incidents are either the product of the
author's imagination or are used factiously, and
any resemblance to actual persons, living or dead,
business establishments, events or locales is
entirely coincidental.

To my readers,
You're wonderful. Thank you for the messages,
emails, comments, surprises, and kindness.

Acknowledgments

Special thanks to my husband, Brad, for being my 'consultant' on this series. His knowledge and expertise, along with his entire phonebook of friends and contacts, has helped lend authenticity to the series.

Thank you to my cover designer, Kerry Prater, for keeping the brothers consistent and realistic.

Thank you to my editor, Lauren Hanson. For making sure West's added commentary was taken out and repaired.

Thank you to Texas Game Warden H. Lutz for explaining rules and regulations and giving some insight into the roles and responsibilities of a warden.

Thank you to Mainstreet Coffee House for all the Iced Mocha Lattes and Bella La Brew for the Iced London Fog Lattes. Delicious liquid fuel that helped power me up on tired days and a quiet atmosphere to knock out some words was super helpful.

H

Chapter One

The trout were biting, always a good sign when the entire day stemmed around fishing, especially on such a beautiful morning. Clint Hastings cast his line out into the shimmering water of the Pecos River, his brothers spread along the banks and in the shallows doing the same. Graham, the man of the weekend, groom-to-be, and oldest of the Hastings brothers sat in a worn lawn chair in the shallows, his line resting in the crook of his chair while he worked on retying one of his lures. "You lose another one?" Calvin, the second oldest of the brothers grinned as he flawlessly cast his line out into the water. Having deemed himself the grandest fisherman of the bunch, Cal patiently waited for the twitch on his line that would inevitably come quicker than Clint's.

"No. I'm swappin' bait," Graham growled, clearly unhappy that he'd had zero luck the entire morning.

"You should just hop on a floaty, Graham," Lawrence teased. "Bask in the sun, even out that farmer's tan. I mean, no use wastin' the bait." Clint grinned as Lawrence ruffled Graham's hair, further annoying him. "Cheer up, bro," Lawrence continued. "Julia's not marrying you for your fishing abilities."

"Thank God," Hayes yelled from the bank, his white smile flashing against his tan skin.

"In fact," Lawrence, with no need for further encouragement, continued ragging on Graham. "I don't really know why she is marryin' you."

"Because of my charming personality," Graham replied flatly, grunting as he poked his finger with his hook.

"That definitely must be it." Philip laughed. "I'm pretty sure that is what everyone knows you for... your charm."

"If it was charm Julia was after, we all know I would have been the one she fell in love with,"

Lawrence bragged. "I mean, I have more than enough to cover all of us."

Clint cleared his throat. "I challenge that, Law."

Lawrence glanced his direction and shrugged. "I'll acquiesce a little to you. You've always had those girls in Sheffield stirred up."
Clint's chummy smile had Seth, the youngest brother, laughing beside him.

"That I do," Clint stated proudly.

"And what a feat," Calvin sarcastically called. "To have charm and no one special to direct it towards. At least Lawrence has Ruby. I have Alice. Graham has Julia. Hayes has Ally. Philip has Helena. What good is charm if you can't woo an amazing woman?"

"Have you ever thought that maybe not all of us want to be in love, Cal?" Clint challenged. "Maybe I like to keep my options open."

"Right." Cal shook his head. "I think the real reason you don't have someone special is that you can't find a woman who can put up with you for long."

The brothers laughed as Clint rolled his eyes and reeled in his line. He waded through the water towards the bank, reaching his hand into the cooler and fetching himself a beer. It was only ten, but they'd been fishing since sun-up. And it was a bachelor party, after all. He plopped into the free chair next to Graham, his ankles settling beneath the water and his feet resting on smooth rocks. "I have hope that one day I'll want to settle down with the right one," Clint continued. "But until then, I'll happily host all the bachelor party weekends like this one on y'all's behalf." He raised his can of beer in a toasting gesture before taking a long and satisfying sip.

"If this weekend is about me, then why is it you're the only one drinking all the beer?" Graham asked.

Clint held his can towards his brother and Graham shook his head.

"That's why. You turn it down. I even made sure I bought your favorite kind. So much for spending the extra money on the fancy stuff." Clint enjoyed his next sip and answered Philip's call to toss him one by reaching into the cooler and scooping one out. He launched it towards his brother and Philip settled it into his pant pocket while he quickly began reeling in whatever tugged on his line.

Clint sighed as he leaned his head back and closed his eyes. The sun speckled behind his eyelids, and he listened to the sounds of his brothers chatting and the shushing of the river as it rolled by in relaxing waves. He needed this trip. After spending the hunting season in New Mexico, the spring burning in February, and cattle work, Clint needed a breather. He also, despite never claiming the fact, had missed his brothers while he was gone all fall and winter. And other than Sunday meals at Annie's, it was rare they all took time off to gather together and just relax. Yes, they had football on Saturdays, but hanging out in the water, a line beneath the surface and hoping for a bite was something they didn't do enough of anymore. When Cal had pitched the idea of a camping, fishing, and hiking bachelor weekend for Graham, Clint fully supported the idea. And he was glad he did. He could tell his brothers needed the break as well, since they rarely left the ranch. But with Doc Wilkenson's help, Alice's dad, they knew their animals were in safe hands while they were away. The old man agreed to feed all the dogs, Graham's cat, and to check on the cattle and horses. He was spending his weekend on the ranch in Graham's house, and banking some extra time with Alice in the bargain. It worked out for everyone. And Julia, Graham's future bride, was relieved not to be on the ranch alone, as she was still adjusting to the remote lifestyle.

Clint finished his beer and slipped the can in the designated trash bag tied to the back of the chair he occupied. Reaching into the cooler again, he grabbed another one along with a protein bar. He needed something to tide him over until lunch, which actually looked promising if they all considered Hayes' stringer. The sun was heating up and he could tell Seth and Lawrence were reaching their limit of fishing. Lawrence reeled his line in and walked back towards the bank and rested his rod against a tree. He then stripped his shirt off and waded out into the water until he was neck deep, dipping his head back to wet his hair and then to fully float on his back.

"Look at Law. He's so used to Ruby doing all his cooking, he thinks he can just float around while we catch his dinner," Philip teased.

Lawrence, his ears slightly submerged in the water, didn't hear the banter and continued to lazily float, his eyes staring up at the sky.

"I don't know." Seth added his own rod next to Lawrence's. "Looks pretty refreshing." He grabbed a floatie and headed towards his older brother, Lawrence coming to attention at the excessive splashing next to him.

Clint reached for his rod and reel again and stood. He grabbed two more beers from the cooler, sliding them into his pant pockets for safe keeping, and then walked knee deep out into the water to try his hand at fishing again. Graham flicked his refreshed line out into the water, his eyes surveying the area, his brothers, and his bait in one quick motion as if he still hadn't relaxed. Not letting his brother's lack of enthusiasm for a break from the ranch tamper his own, Clint flicked his wrist, sending his line out over the water in one smooth motion.

~

Bailey Keller adjusted and tucked the tail of her shirt into her pants as she climbed out of her work truck and began the trek towards the sounds of masculine laughter. She'd worked her way up and down the Pecos all morning checking on all outdoorsmen. As one of the few Texas game wardens that covered this particular county, she made a regular habit of checking in on the Pecos area. Campers, hunters, hikers, and anglers were, for the most part, responsible in picking up after themselves and following guidelines set by the state. But every now and then there were a few bad apples. Bad apples tended to rotten even more so when they had a woman writing them up a ticket for violating the law. Sometimes their anger made her nervous, but for the most part, her badge rendered respect.

She stepped through the clearing and watched as seven men, all tall in stature with various muscular builds fished for trout. It looked to be a campsite set up, tidy except for a few pairs of wet clothing draped on rope lines or tree limbs. One man sat nearest the bank, his broad shoulders already tinged pink from the morning sun. He seemed unaware of her presence. Another man, ankle deep in the water glanced her direction at her movement and froze temporarily before his line snagged and he quickly began reeling in his catch. He spoke something to the seated man, the latter one turning to peek over his shoulder. He rested his rod to the side of his chair and stood. Her eyes, though appreciative of the handsome build and face, tried to hide their surprise at the height and breadth of him. She inwardly prayed he was friendly because going up against this man would be like poking a giant grizzly. "Morning," she greeted warmly. "Warden Keller." She extended her hand, and he shook it firmly, his large palm swallowing her small hand. "Nice set up you have here."

"We think so," the man replied, briefly flashing a gaze over the other men.

"You gentlemen out for the weekend?"

"Yes ma'am. Been here since last night."

She nodded. "You chose a good spot."

He rested his hands on his hips as he waited for her to get to the point.

"I'm making rounds today because we've had some violators fishing over limits and without a license. I'm going to need to see everyone's fishing licenses."

"Not a problem." The man barked towards the closest compatriot. "Gather them up, Cal."

The man walked towards a backpack hanging on a post and fished inside for a wallet. Opening the worn leather sides, he pulled out a folded piece of paper and handed it to her. She looked it over and up at him. "Thank you, Mr. Hastings."

Seth, always nervous about breaking any rules, hurried to fetch his license as well. He handed it to her, and she nodded in acceptance. "Another Mr. Hastings." She smiled warmly as she handed it back to the young man.

"We're all Hastings, ma'am," he replied. "We're brothers."

"Ah, well, this must be a nice family trip then." She accepted Philip's next and looked it over.

"Bachelor party weekend for my brother." Seth thumbed over his shoulder towards the first man she'd encountered, Graham Hastings. "He marries his sweetheart in a couple weeks."

"Hastings..." Bailey looked up at the next brother. "Are you the Hastings family that owns the 7H Ranch over in Parks?"

Calvin tipped his hat as he handed her his license. "That we are. Don't believe we've seen you out there before."

"I'm new to this county." She thanked him for his license and looked up to see a shirtless Lawrence dripping wet and attempting to thumb through his wallet with damp fingers.

"Clint! Come on now! Warden needs to see your license!" Seth yelled towards the last remaining brother in the water, the man slowly trudging his way towards her. He set his rod down and crossed his arms over his wide, bare chest. The youngest Hastings tapped his arm. "Come on now, show it to her."

"No."

At his rude and defiant response, the other brothers' heads snapped up and to attention.

"I'm sorry?" Bailey asked. "I just need to take a quick look and make sure everyone has the correct licensing to be fishing up here."

"Clearly we do." Clint waved at his other brothers.

"*They* do, yes. I'm still waiting to see if *you* do as well."

"Clint, just show her your license." Graham barked, stalking over to the fire pit and adding some logs. One of the other brothers helped get the fire started, apparently the preparation of what would be their soon-to-be cooking headquarters for lunch.

Bailey waited patiently, though her insides started tightening at what looked to be an unpleasant standoff with the handsome man in front of her.

"I shouldn't have to show her my license," Clint replied. "I fish here all the time. I've never run into problems with the wardens. Do you know who we are?" he asked her, arrogance ringing in his tone. She also caught the faint whiff of alcohol, a smell she hadn't noticed on any of the other brothers. Dread settled in her stomach.

"Sir, I understand you may frequently fish on the Pecos, and we are a bit understaffed so there may not be a warden passing through when you do. But I am passing through right now, and by law, to fish in this river, you have to have a state of Texas fishing license with you. If you need to fetch it from your vehicle, I do not mind waiting. If you do not have one, then—"

"You will *not* write me a ticket." Clint stepped towards her and though she wanted to, she did not retreat one inch. Instead, she angled her chin a little higher to meet his eyes.

"Sir, I'm simply doing my job and asking to look at a piece of paper. That's all."

"And what exactly is that? Your job?" Clint mouthed.

Bailey straightened her shoulders. "Sir, need I remind you that Texas Game Wardens have the same authority as any other form of law enforcement? I am here to make sure that the Texas Parks and Wildlife Code and the Texas Penal Code are consistently being followed. There are also proclamations enacted by the Parks and Wildlife Commission under authority delegated by the legislature that you are required, by law, to follow when hunting, fishing, or camping on state property."

One of the brothers placed a restraining hand on the man's arm and he jerked it free in a vigorous yank that was too much for his balance. He stumbled forward on his own volition, bumping into Bailey. Without hesitancy, she spun him around in one fluid motion, placing handcuffs on his wrists and forcing him to sit. "What the— You can't cuff me! I haven't done anything!"

"Shut it, Clint!" Graham barked. "Look, Warden Keller, my younger brother is a mouth, a nuisance, and a jerk, and I apologize. He clearly didn't bring his license with him. He probably forgot since he was planning all the other details of this trip. Now,

I'm not makin' excuses for his behavior, but I am going to ask you for a favor."

"He will still receive a written violation," Bailey stated firmly.

"Oh, no doubt. And I understand and respect that. I'm just asking that you get to it pretty quick if you don't mind. Because my idiot brother is only going to get worse with that mouth and I don't want to bail him out of jail for something stupid."

"He's been drinking?" she asked.

"Oh yeah," Calvin replied. "We've got him under control though. Promise."

"Intimidating law enforcement isn't exactly a positive reflection on his character in this matter."

"Intimidating law enforce—" Clint started to grumble and stand, but Lawrence kicked his ankle out from under him, sending him back to a sitting position on the dirt.

"Not a word, ya dummy," Lawrence mouthed.

Bailey reached into her pocket and withdrew her pad and began filling out the ticket and violation. "If you can ensure that he will not illegally fish without a license the remainder of the weekend, I will not force you gentlemen to pack up camp. If I or another Warden come by to check and he is fishing, all of you will be ticketed then. Understood?"

"Yes ma'am. And trust me, he won't be a problem." Graham's harsh tone and narrowed eyes on his brother told her that he would definitely be under his older brother's thumb the remainder of the trip.

She tore the ticket off the pad and held it out to Clint. He stared at it. "How am I supposed to grab it with my hands cuffed behind my back?" His lips quirked in an arrogant smile. Philip reached out and snatched it from her hand, slapped his brother on the back of the head, and then helped him to his feet. Bailey uncuffed him, taking a cautious step away from his fuming face.

"You gentlemen have a safe rest of the weekend."

Graham tipped his hat, as did a few of the other brothers as she walked away. Once out of sight, she heard the ranting anger of Clint Hastings through the trees.

H

Chapter Two

"*I'm sorry I doubted* you." Julia McComas glanced up with a loving, admiring gaze at Graham and then rested her head against his arm as they stared out over the luscious green pasture that would, in a couple of weeks, host their wedding. "I can't believe that burning the grass would produce such a beautiful result."

"Beautiful things take time to create."

A throat cleared behind them and Clint rolled his eyes as Graham turned around. "You done being sappy, bro?"

Julia laughed and squeezed Graham's arm. "Don't listen to him, Graham. He's just jealous." She winked at Clint and he, along with Lawrence next to him, nodded.

"Who wouldn't be, Jewels?" Lawrence replied. "You're a catch."

"Well, thank you, Lawrence. Now, if you boys will excuse me—"

"Wait—" Lawrence held up his hand. "You're not going to spill the beans about your bachelorette weekend? What do you ladies have planned?"

Julia grinned. "Why should I tell you boys?"

"Come on, Julia. You can't torture us like that. Right, Graham?"

Graham smirked as he leaned down and kissed his bride-to-be on the lips. "Have fun."

"I will. I assure you that none of us will be handcuffed." She narrowed her gaze at Clint, and he shrugged.

"You sure about that?" Lawrence asked. "You do have Al and Ruby plannin' your weekend. Who knows? Maybe handcuffs will show up." Lawrence wriggled his hips and lassoed the air in a suggestive dance move that would have been inappropriate had it not been for his lack of rhythm and sloppy steps. "With 'law enforcement.'" He made air-quotations with his fingers, and Julia laughed.

"No stripper shenanigans for this girl. Not my kind of party." She slid an arm around Graham's waist for one last squeeze. "I love you."

"Love you." He hesitantly released her as an annoyed Alice honked her horn again and leaned out her truck window.

"You're marryin' him in like two weeks, Julia! Get in the car so we can go have fun!"

Ruby pumped her fist in the air and hooted in celebration, blowing a quick kiss to Lawrence.

Clint laughed as his brothers watched longingly as Alice, like a bat out of the depths of Hades, zoomed down the dirt drive. "I'm surprised Calvin wasn't here to give Al one last farewell kiss."

"He already did." Lawrence, with a satisfied grin, glanced towards their brother's house. "He and I met up with Ruby and Alice when he was checking Alice's oil before they left. We got our smooches in early."

"Pathetic," Clint harrumphed as he crossed his arms.

"You hear that, Graham?" Lawrence shook his head in disappointment. "Just because Clint's not gettin' smooches, he's all sour towards us."

"It happens even to the greatest of men. Jealousy is a tough pill to swallow," Graham mumbled.

"Jealous?" Clint, baffled, held up his hands. "What makes you think I'm jealous?"

"Well, for starters, you were sweet on Kara up at the diner and now she's datin' Jimmy. You missed out on that one. And then we're all finding incredible women one after another and you're just... there." Lawrence pointed to where Clint stood.

"Again, maybe I'm not looking right now. Besides, I'm going to be busy getting the hunting operation up and running. I won't have time for datin', or smoochin', or cuddlin'. I'll be working."

Lawrence and Graham both laughed at that news.

"It happens," Clint said. "Especially if I'm working on hunting."

"Right. Well, you have fun with that." Lawrence pointed towards his truck. "I'm heading up to my place. I need to tweak my fence. Dang dog keeps escaping and runnin' around this whole ranch looking for me and stirrin' up trouble."

Clint watched as Lawrence pulled away and Graham began walking to his truck. Now was his chance to talk more with Graham about his hunting operation plans and the proposed budget he had in mind. The subject, a sensitive one, never seemed to be discussed due to Graham's lack of interest. He had agreed to let Clint try it, which in itself was a huge feat, but Graham also never had time to talk more about it. His subtle way of putting it off. "Hey, Graham. If you have a minute, I wanted to talk to you about the operation." He jogged to catch up to his brother's long strides. Graham paused at his truck and turned, patiently waiting for Clint to continue. "I wanted to check and see when would be a good time to go over my plans with you."

"We've gone over your plans," Graham said. "I'm ready to see some action behind them."

Clint flinched at the harsh tone. "I've been waiting on you."

"What for? I'm not working it. This is your project," Graham added.

"Well, yeah, I know. I meant I wasn't sure what kind of budget you were going to give me to get it started. Everything sort of hinges on that."

"You've yet to bring me your numbers. How can I allocate a budget if I don't know what the needs are?"

Clint blew a frustrated breath. "I told you all of this months ago."

"You told me, yes. You haven't *shown* me, Clint. I need to see it on paper. You can't just have ideas floatin' around in your head and expect me to fork over the money. I need to see a fully executed management plan, costs, projected profit—"

"Again, I went over this with you months ago." Clint crossed his arms over his chest and squared his jaw, trying to contain his temper.

"Then give me your plans. You can leave them at the house." Graham hoisted himself into his truck and shut the door. He draped his elbow on the open windowsill. "Need to check water troughs today when you're done poutin'."

"I'm not poutin' and I'm not checking troughs today. I'm headed over to Sanderson."

"What for?"

"I'm meeting with the state wildlife biologist that covers this area."

Graham's brows rose slightly behind his sunglasses.

"Yeah, *doing* something," Clint stressed.

"Well, let me know how that goes." Graham's tone grew lighter and more agreeable at the news of Clint executing part of his hunting operation plans. His brother shifted into drive and headed towards the main dirt road of the ranch and Clint watched as his taillights disappeared. A man of action, that's what Graham respected. That's also what Graham didn't believe Clint could be. But he wanted this. He wanted to find his foothold on the ranch and hunting was it. He loved hunting. The entire hunting season spent in New Mexico had shown him the opportunity he had, as well as the potential the 7H could achieve. Determined, Clint hustled over to his own pickup and headed towards Sanderson. If Graham wanted a written management plan, Mike was the man to help with that.

~

She was hardly ever in the office. Most of her time was spent traveling the four counties she and her fellow wardens covered. So, to be seated at a desk reviewing the latest legislation changes wasn't exactly the type of day she'd planned on having. She wanted and *needed* to be outdoors. Bailey grew up outside, or at least, that's what her dad always told people. She was typically covered in mud, wrestling an animal of some sort, or swimming in the pond out behind their house... naked, which at five years old was considered funny. She even remembered her mom tossing her a bar of soap one day while she was out there. She loved the outdoors. And since she'd now grown out of her feisty five-year-old habits of swimming naked in the pond, she found she spent her time working or hiking in her spare time just to get her fix of open air. Anything to be outdoors. It was no surprise to her parents that she chose the profession she did. Though they worried over her safety, they knew she was in the right field.

The words on her computer screen blurred and she blinked a couple of times before reaching for the hair tie around her wrist and hastily smoothing her hair into a short ponytail. She liked keeping her hair on the shorter side. Chin length suited her narrow face, and the strawberry blonde seemed less bright and cheerful and more serious when kept cut in sharp edges that framed her cheeks. It also made her look older, she hoped, as the freckles across her nose and upper cheeks seemed to confuse people about her age. She'd been a Texas game warden for five years, but most people thought she was green. She was young, yes, but it wasn't her first rodeo. And she knew her stuff. She knew the laws. She knew the areas she was assigned. She also loved the land and felt honored to do her part in protecting it while also enjoying it.

"Keller." She looked up to see a fellow warden, Tom Cates, staring at her. "I've been sayin' your name for five minutes."

"Sorry," she sighed, swiveling her chair to face him. "I was lost in the statutes."

"I heard you wrangled the Hastings brothers this weekend. How'd that go?"

She lifted a brow. "You know them?"

He smirked. "Pretty much everyone does. Their ranch is pretty well-known. I hear you interrupted a bachelor weekend for the oldest brother, Graham. That is not a man I enjoy tangling with."

"He was nice," Bailey replied. "I had no trouble out of him or the others, minus the one I ticketed."

"You ticketed one of them?" Tom's eyes widened. "For what?"

"He didn't have his fishing license."

He laughed. "Wow. You are strict, aren't you?"

She nodded. "Yes."

"Which brother was it?" Tom asked curiously.

"Clay? Clyde? Something like that." Bailey struggled to remember.

"Clint?"

"That's the one." She snapped her fingers and nodded. "He was a bit tipsy as well, which didn't help matters."

"Again, it was a bachelor party weekend."

She shrugged her shoulders. "Still have to follow the law. And all his brothers had their licenses, so he should have had his. Simple as that."

Tom leaned back in his computer chair, the small creak from the gears grinding under his weight. He crossed his ankles and rested them on a filing cabinet.

"And I don't like arrogance. I don't care who they are or what their name is. He tried to play that card, but he quickly realized I didn't care."

Tom snickered. "Well, I have to be in Parks in a couple of days. Ride with me. We'll make the rounds together. We'll swing by the 7H so you can see the place."

"Why would we need to swing by there?"

"I tend to pop in on them when I'm in the area. Keeps up good relations."

"I see. Well, I'll think about it." She pointed to her computer. "But I should finish this first. The faster I'm done reading all this, the quicker I can get out of here."

Tom took the hint and nodded, dropping his feet to the floor and walking across the room to another warden's desk to chat. Bailey wasn't sure if he'd read the new legislation changes yet or not, but he didn't seem too concerned about them. She, however, was. Anything new required proper study and attention to make sure she could execute her job precisely and perfectly. Or, as perfect as she could, anyway, and preferably without the use of handcuffs.

She glanced up again when she heard Tom's overly cheerful greeting in response to the bell above the door. A man, tall, broad-shouldered, dressed in a pressed shirt and jeans with his cowboy hat pulled low, tugged the door closed behind him. When he glanced up, her back stiffened. Clint Hastings. His eyes roamed the room and landed on her, his lips tilting in a small smirk before his attention went toward Tom. A handshake, a hearty hello, and then those long legs were traipsing their way toward her desk. She straightened in her chair when he sat across from her.

"Warden," he greeted, removing his hat and placing it on his knee. He smoothed a quick hand over his short hair before leaning comfortably back against the chair.

"Mr. Hastings." She placed her hands in her lap to keep him from seeing them jitter. "What can I do for you?"

"Well, I don't really need you to do anything." He flashed a quick, handsome smile before continuing. "I was over in Sanderson visiting with Mike."

"The wildlife biologist?" she asked.

He nodded. "Yes. And he encouraged me to come on by and meet the wardens that now cover the area I live in… said there were some new faces. I'm assuming he meant yours now that I'm here."

"I see. And why did he feel you needed to meet the wardens?"

"As a goodwill measure, good manners sort of thing. See, I'm planning on starting a commercial huntin' operation on our ranch this season, and well, I want to be on good terms with local law enforcement. I also wanted to see if you'd have any suggestions for me."

"Suggestions?"

"You know, any new rules and regulations I need to be aware of."

"You don't even follow the current rules and regulations."

Clint tilted his head, his eyes narrowing slightly as he took the insult in stride. "That was one time, thank you, and I believe I already paid that ticket, even though I didn't want to. Thankfully, my brother Hayes convinced me I should. And yes, in the past I was the brother who liked testing the boundaries of the rules. I'm not that guy anymore."

"Really?" She crossed her arms and studied him a moment.

"Well, not all the time." His sly smirk had her heart fluttering a moment and she inwardly scolded herself for having a moment of awareness at a handsome face. "But I have to start this off on the right foot so that Graham, my brother, will see that it is viable and worth our time and investment."

"Sounds like you're serious about it."

"I am. I spent all last season in New Mexico working on various ranches as a guide to learn all I could. I just met with Mike to see what I needed in order to get some private land tags. Seems I'm a couple years away from being able to do that, but that's not a big deal. I can wait on it."

"You definitely have your work cut out for you."

"Yep, but again, I'm ready for it. Mike's going to come out and help me draft up a wildlife management plan and we're going to get started on the right foot... which is why I'm here. I want to have a good relationship with you guys, so that if any issues arise, we can work it out."

"Without handcuffs?" Bailey asked.

"Preferably." Clint's cheeks slightly blushed and he dropped his blue gaze a moment, rubbing his hand over his chin. "I apologize for that, by the way. I was bein' stupid. I have a tendency to pop off when I'm aggravated. I'm workin' on that. My brothers ripped me a new one over it too. And when Annie finds out..."

She didn't know who Annie was, but Clint seemed to sober up at the thought of disappointing her. Maybe this Annie was his girlfriend. He didn't wear a ring, so he wasn't married. Then again, some ranchers didn't wear rings for fear of getting them caught in equipment and losing a finger. So maybe he was. She didn't know. But this Annie woman seemed to have a high standard to be held, and Clint seemed keen to meet it. She already liked the woman. "Anyway," he continued. "I apologize for lashing out at you and being unruly. It won't happen again."

"Thanks." Bailey offered a satisfied smile. "Clean slate."

"Thanks." He smiled, the dimple in his cheek flashing along with the one in his chin. He had a nice smile, she noticed that about all the brothers that day on the river. They were all the epitome of handsome cowboy. But there was something about Clint's broad stance when he stood that captivated her. She shook away the thought as she found her feet and extended her hand. "Nice of you to come in, Mr. Hastings."

He shook it, his wide palm rough from years of work. "Just call me Clint. Have a good one, Warden Keller. And if you're ever in Parks, stop on by the 7H. I'll show ya around." He slid his hat back onto his head, waved to the few remaining wardens, and walked out, her eyes following him through the slatted window blinds until she saw him back out of the parking lot.

H

Chapter Three

"And what will it be?" Kara asked, pen and pad in hand as she waited for Bailey to decide what suited her fancy. Tom, having ordered a patty melt sandwich, waited with hungry eyes as he watched the cook come out of the kitchen and deliver dishes to a nearby table.

"I'll have the Parks burger. All the way." Bailey handed her menu to the pretty waitress and watched as she scribbled it on her pad.

"Good choice. I'll have these out in a few." She hurried away and stopped briefly at a table to snatch away empty plates on her way back to the kitchen.

"They're busy."

"Always. Sloppy's Diner is a must stop when passing through Parks. Ol' Sloppy isn't here today, though. Heard she's on a bachelorette weekend with Graham Hastings' future bride, which would make sense since Sloppy is engaged to his younger brother, Lawrence," Tom explained.

"And her name is Sloppy?" Bailey asked, curious as to why anyone would name their child such a name.

"Nah. Though I couldn't tell ya what her real name is. I don't know her that well. Cute thing, though."

The bell above the door jingled and in walked a group of women babbling and smiling, dressed as if they were from out of town in stylish dresses, flawless faces, and confident steps.

"There she is now." He pointed to a spunky, raven-haired woman with purple sneakers and a yellow sundress.

They watched as she hurried to the counter and spoke with the waitress and then ducked under the bar door and began filling to-go cups with teas and sodas.

"My bet is that would be the bachelorette crew." Tom gave a low whistle under his breath. "Not a bad lookin' one in the bunch."

A man walked into the diner, his cowboy hat slung hastily on his head, and his shirt covered in dust. His gaze found the group of women and he hurried towards them. One of the women turned around and embraced him, no cares about his dirty appearance. Tom stood and walked towards the group, the man turning when the women notified him of someone behind him. "Philip Hastings." Tom extended his hand. "Good to see you."

"Tom," Philip smiled in greeting and pumped the warden's hand. "What brings you to Parks?"

Tom thumbed over his shoulder towards Bailey. "Showing the new warden the area a bit. We planned to venture out to the 7H this afternoon. Your brothers around?"

"A few of them. Fridays can be hit or miss, but Graham is no doubt out there." He looked to a pretty brunette. "Julia, Graham on the ranch today?"

"He is." She smiled and walked forward, her eyes surveying the warden's uniform. "Everything alright?"

Philip chuckled. "Graham is fine." He looked to the warden. "Right?"

"Oh yeah," Tom smiled. "Just wanted to make sure someone was out there if we made the trip."

Julia's gaze fluttered over the man's shoulder towards Bailey. She walked over and took Tom's vacant seat. "I'm Julia McComas. You new in town?"

Bailey, surprised by the woman's warmth, shook her head. "I live over in Sanderson, but I'm new to the area as far as work."

"Are you the warden that handcuffed, Clint?" Another woman, a blonde with a messy up-do sauntered over, sipping on one of the to-go cups the black-haired beauty whipped together.

Bailey forced herself not to feel foolish over such a comment. "I am."

"Good for you." The woman toasted towards her. "Name's Alice Wilkenson." She pulled an empty chair from the neighboring table without asking its occupants if it was taken. Julia scolded with a look and Alice shrugged. "What? No one's sitting in it. Cool to see a woman game warden around here."

Bailey looked up as her waitress returned with their meals and slid them onto the table. "Thanks, Kara," Julia said, and turned her attention back towards Bailey. "So, what's your name?"

"Bailey Keller."

"Nice to meet you." Julia waved a hand towards Philip. "Sorry your partner got hijacked, but Philip likes to talk."

"One of the things I love about him." Another woman walked up, forcing Alice to scoot halfway off her chair so she could share the borrowed chair. "I'm Helena Shaw. Philip's my boyfriend."

"And you must be the woman Graham is engaged to?" Bailey asked, looking at Julia.

She flushed in pure pleasure. "I am."

"God have mercy on her soul," Alice mumbled, and accepted the slap to the shoulder from Julia with a laugh.

"Stop it, be nice."

"I am nice," Alice defended. "Bailey has had the unfortunate pleasure of runnin' into Graham. I bet he thoroughly enjoyed your presence at his bachelor camping trip," she smirked. "I really do want all the details."

"Oh, I—"

"Alice," Julia chided. "give her a break. Besides, Graham assured me he was respectful. He was respectful, right?" She narrowed her gaze on Bailey and Bailey nodded. "Good." Appeased, Julia glanced up as Sloppy walked forward with a drink for Julia and herself.

"This is Ruby. She owns the diner," Julia introduced, and the petite woman waved with enthusiasm. "We're on our way to Fort Stockton for my bachelorette weekend. We're just waiting on one more friend to join us."

The bell above the door jingled again and a loud hoot and holler from an elderly woman dressed in a bright floral dress swooped inside, a floppy sun hat resting on her crisp, white hair. "I'm ready, girls!"

Alice choked on her drink and muttered an "Oh, Lord," before the older woman walked up, her eyes already roaming over Bailey's features. "Well, well, well, who do we have here?"

"This is Bailey Keller," Julia introduced. "She's one of the new game wardens for the area."

"The one who arrested Clint," Alice reported.

"Arrested?!" The woman held a hand over her heart.

"Oops." Alice realized her blunder and grimaced.

"Now what in the world did Clint do?" The woman pointed to an empty chair at a nearby table. "Honey, you using that?" The man shook his head, and she whipped the chair around faster than a slap to the cheek. "Honey, you tell me what that boy did to get arrested."

Bailey waved her hands. "No, no, no... there must be a mix up. I didn't arrest him."

"You did wrestle him into some handcuffs though." Alice nodded in approval. "And I would have loved to have seen that." She laughed and Ruby rolled her eyes.

"Cut him some slack. He's under a lot of stress right now," Ruby defended.

"Stress my—"

"Alice Wilkenson, just stop right there," the older woman interrupted, and Alice bit her tongue in obedience.

"I apologize, but I can't discuss the matter with someone not party to—"

"Then I'll elucidate for ya, Annie," Alice interrupted proudly, no doubt ready to elaborate more than necessary.

"Good grief, she is so much like Lawrence," Ruby whispered to Julia and Helena. She jumped at the slap on her thigh from Alice.

"Annie?" Bailey looked to the older woman. "*You're* Annie?"

"Yes ma'am, I am."

"I see." Bailey couldn't help the smile that washed over her face at the thought of the big Clint Hastings being scared of such a little old woman. "Clint mentioned you the other day."

"Oh, did he?" Annie's brow rose. "Well, if it was about sneakin' around and not telling me about his bad behavior, you can bet he's got another thing comin'. Those boys know better than to disrespect the law. Now, you tell me what that boy did."

"He didn't have his fishing license," Julia reported. "And he received a ticket."

"After throwin' a hissy fit that landed him in handcuffs," Alice added with pleasure.

"Well, good for you." Annie patted Bailey's arm. "He knows better than to act like an ape. That boy—" She shook her head in disappointment.

"Please don't be hard on him, ma'am," Bailey defended. "He did come by the office the other day to apologize."

"Did he now?" Annie's right brow quirked again at that news and she and the other women exchanged curious expressions.

"Well, another strong female presence in Parks." Annie grinned conspiratorially at the other women. "I think I'm growin' quite spoiled."

"We're the spoiled ones." Helena patted Annie's hand and she looked up as Philip and Tom walked towards the table.

"I guess our time is up." Annie sighed in regret. "I was just getting to know the newest Rosie in town."

"Rosie?" whispered Ruby in question to Alice.

"The Riveter," Alice explained. "Strong woman."

Ruby grinned and flashed a quick wink at Bailey.

"I like her." Annie hugged Philip and patted Tom on the arm. "We need all the women we can get around here." She stood and gathered her purse. "Well, girls, are we going to party yet or just linger around this dusty ol' town?"

"She acts like she never goes anywhere." Alice and Helena stood, Helena smoothing a hand over the front of her dress.

"I've got Henry out at the ranch with Hayes for the weekend, so I'm free to roam without worryin' over him."

"Speaking of Hayes," Julia looked to Alice. "are we picking up Ally on the way?"

"No. She's meeting us there. She was waiting for her mom to get into town to watch Ava, and then she was going to head to the hotel."

"Oh, good." Annie clasped her hands together in pride. "All my girls together. This is going to be so much fun." She squealed the last of the words and squeezed Philip one more time. "Love you, boy. Now make sure those brothers of yours don't get my Henry into trouble."

Philip tapped the rim of his hat. "Yes ma'am."

"It was nice to meet you all." Bailey stood in farewell as the women bustled around moving chairs back, grabbing purses and drinks, and chattering back and forth. They seemed like a fun group, and she wondered how they'd all come to be such good friends.

"Ten bucks Clint gets arrested again today," Alice stated on her way to the door.

Ruby laughed. "Give it up, Alice. Just because you want to see him behind bars for kicks, doesn't mean you should wish it on him."

'Trust me, it wouldn't be his first time. Remember when he egged Coach Simpson's house, Annie?"

"Do not remind me." Annie hustled them out the door with Alice recounting Clint's mischievous deeds behind them.

Philip exhaled a long breath. "They're a lot to take in when they're all together." He laughed and shook Tom's hand. "Good to see you, Tom. And welcome to the area, Warden Keller."

"Thank you. Good to see you, again."

"Likewise. And hey, if you ever have any trouble out of any of my brothers, just let Annie know. She's better than the sheriff at striking fear into us."

Bailey nodded. "I'm sure you will all be law-abiding citizens from here on out."

"With the threat of callin' Annie, you betcha." Philip nodded his farewell as he walked out of the diner and up the sidewalk towards the feed store.

"Welcome to Parks." Breathlessly, Tom found his seat. "Where the Hastings men *and* women are everywhere."

~

Clint had just removed his hat and set it on the designated shelf next to his back door that housed not only his work hat but various shapes, colors, and styles of other hats he used every time he walked out of the house. His boots, of different varieties as well, were lined up beneath it. One of his greatest memories was of his grandfather having a similar set up when he was still alive and living in Graham's house. Though Graham had remodeled the inside of the house a decade or so ago, Clint remembered the hat shelf clearly, always enamored with his grandfather's collection. There was a single cowboy hat on a display stand on his fireplace mantle, a grey felt hat that remained crisp around the edges. It was his grandfather's church hat, and Clint's favorite growing up. It now sat in a place of honor in his house to serve as a reminder of the hardworking man that wore it. Despite what his brothers thought, Clint had fond memories of growing up on the ranch, and he loved the place. He didn't intend to leave the place either, though he was pretty sure Lawrence and Calvin had a bet on when he would officially throw in the towel. Not that they wanted him to, though he knew Graham wouldn't mind the headache of his presence disappearing every now and then. But all Clint needed was his own niche. His own project on the ranch. He'd spent his entire life working his grandfather's, father's, and Graham's vision for the ranch. He wanted to work his own.

Hayes had done it. Hayes created his horse stables, pens, and business from nothing, and now that's most of what he did. He helped with cows, sure, and clearing if need be, but Hayes' time and heart went to his horses. And everyone respected him for it. Graham had the cattle, Calvin his machines, Lawrence the land, and Seth… well, Seth had yet to find his place too. Philip had the store in town where he felt needed, wanted, and productive off the ranch like he wanted, so why did everyone give Clint flack about wanting to do his own thing on the ranch as well?

His excitement over establishing a hunting operation only deepened after talking to the state biologist. Mike was going to be his biggest asset in the months to come. He didn't laugh at Clint's ideas. He didn't mock his lack of knowledge on a few key points, instead, he helped him. He explained what needed to be done, in detail. Clint was grateful for his time because now he knew what he needed to add to his plan before presenting it to Graham. And after stopping to talk to the wardens, especially Warden Keller, he felt he now had solid footing with them. Hopefully. The spirited blonde warden seemed wound pretty tight, but she seemed to be surprised and pleased he'd stopped by to apologize. He could tell she tried to hide her pleasure, but her eyes had brightened a few times during their conversation, and he noticed her nervous hands in her lap even though she'd tried to hide those too. He smiled thinking about her handcuffing him at the Pecos River. She'd reacted quick as a mouse and before he knew it, his knees were in the dirt. He'd never been thrown for such a loop by a woman. And definitely not by one who was a quarter his size. He'd give her props for that. But he also kind of wanted to see what else the little firecracker had up her sleeve. *Little Firecracker*. Yep, that was now going to be her nickname. He liked it. And he had a feeling he hadn't seen anything yet from Warden Bailey Keller.

A horn honked outside his house, and he peeked through the blinds to see Lawrence's truck angled in his drive. Clint grabbed his hat and stepped out onto the porch. "What is it?"

"Wardens are here."

"Interesting," Clint muttered under his breath. "For what?" he yelled over Lawrence's engine.

"Don't know. Graham just called and told me to round everybody up to meet at the main house. He wants us all there to, and I quote, 'make a better impression.' Pretty sure he means you, stupid."

Clint sighed and slipped his boots back on. "I'm comin'."

"Where's Seth?"

"Probably your place or at the garden by Graham's. He planned to uproot some of his squash and zucchini plants today. Refresh things."

"Got it." Lawrence switched gears and headed back the direction he came. Clint watched as he braked as Calvin, driving a skid steer up the dirt road from one of the far pastures, passed by in front of him. Graham had rallied the troops, and like all good leaders, his troops followed orders and made their way to him. Clint pushed back as often as he could to remind Graham that he wasn't the boss of him, though his oldest brother fit the role well. Clint wouldn't let him have that compliment from him, though. But Graham had held their family together. He was the glue now that their parents were gone. And he'd taken the lead at a young age. He owed a lot to Graham, they all did. But Graham also needed the push back from his brothers every now and then to remind him that he didn't have to have it together *all the time*. To relax. However, since Julia had come along, his brother had transformed. He wasn't as strict, bossy, or broody. He'd opened up, laughed more, smiled more, relaxed more. And was slowly becoming a friend again to his brothers. They all owed Julia more than she knew.

He climbed into his truck and took the short drive to Graham's house, the white frame a beacon amongst the grass and dust of the ranch. He saw the game warden's vehicle parked out front and watched as Bailey Keller climbed out of the passenger side and Tom Cates the driver seat.

"Well, well, well..." he muttered, and flashed a quick smile as he pulled in next to them and saw the surprise on her face. She masked it quickly, but he liked that she wasn't expecting him and the small trip to her steps on the grass when he'd distracted her. She recovered smoothly, but he immediately noticed the rod that replaced her backbone at his presence. And now, he was determined more than ever to remove it. He slipped out of the truck and tipped his hat. "Warden Keller."

"Mr. Hastings," she greeted calmly.

"Can't get enough of me, huh?"

"Excuse me?" she balked, and he grinned.

"Kidding." Clint waved for her to head up Graham's steps. "Welcome to the 7H."

The screen door opened, Calvin stepping out and holding it open with the toe of his boot as he shook Tom's hand and then Bailey's as they walked inside. The dining area was crowded, but Graham, in true host form, had a pitcher of cold iced tea on the table with several glasses full of ice waiting for company.

Seth stumbled in through the mudroom door, placing his work gloves on the kitchen counter and quickly washing his hands. Graham nodded in approval at his timing.

"Not a bad welcome wagon." Tom smiled in greeting. "Stopped by Sloppy's for lunch and bumped into Philip in town. He wasn't too sure we'd see all of you out here. We also saw your women headed out of town."

"Already wreaking havoc on Parks." Hayes shook his head on a laugh. "Look out Fort Stockton."

Graham smirked and sat in his chair at the head of the table, everyone following suit and finding a seat.

"This here is Warden Bailey Keller," Tom introduced. "She's new to the coverage area in our counties. I'm just taking her around. I know you all have been somewhat introduced." Tom couldn't help the laugh that bubbled up, and Clint could see Bailey didn't appreciate it.

"I'm afraid that was my fault," Clint interrupted. "I didn't exactly make her job easy that day."

"Do you ever make anyone's job easy?" Calvin teased.

Seth laughed at his brother's comment and Lawrence agreed with the shake of his head.

"We all have our role," Clint added.

Graham listened and then turned towards Tom. "Good to see you both... again."

"Thought we could get a ride around for a bit. Would love to see what you've done with the place the last couple years," Tom stated, waiting for Graham to give a nod of approval.

The oldest brother stood, and everyone followed suit. "I think we can manage that."

Clint watched as Bailey followed his brother outside and everyone lingered on the porch and around the front steps as Graham described a few of their latest projects, specifically the burning for his upcoming wedding. Bailey glanced Clint's direction and he smiled, watching as she quickly diverted her gaze back to his brother. Whatever his plans were for the day, Clint was changing them. Because there was no way he was going to miss riding alongside Bailey Keller and making her fidget some more.

"I'll tag along," Clint answered Graham as his oldest brother had pitched the invite to anyone else. Clint walked by Bailey and patted her on the shoulder. "I promise not to get too rowdy, Warden Keller."

Tom hooted in laughter as Clint opened the back passenger door of Graham's truck for her and watched as she collected herself, hiding her annoyance before climbing inside the vehicle.

"What is he up to?" Calvin leaned over to Hayes and Lawrence as Clint tapped the brim of his hat towards them and grinned.

"I think he likes her." Lawrence, amused, crossed his arms and watched as Graham backed out of his front yard.

"Clint and a law enforcement woman... yeah, that doesn't ring of success." Hayes shook his head.

"Yeah, well, you never know." Lawrence shrugged. "The love bug has bitten us all lately. And if Alice and Cal can find it together, then maybe Clint can find it where he least expects it."

"Why is it so weird to people that Al and I are happy together? You were all the ones pushing us towards one another in the first place." Cal looked perplexed at his brothers.

"You're just too sweet, Cal." Lawrence patted him on the back. "And Al, well, she isn't. I guess we all thought she'd chew you up and spit you out. Or worse, just stomp ya to death. But to our surprise, you've turned her into mush."

Cal grinned at that. "Don't tell her that or she will chew me up."

Hayes laughed as his cell phone rang. "Speaking of women who are little pistols, Ava is calling me it would seem. It's her first time away from Ally in a long time."

"How's that going?" Lawrence asked. "You know, having a kid in the mix?"

"Fine." Hayes answered with a cheerful greeting. "Hey there, butter bean." He walked away from his brothers and was already laughing at whatever little Ava was reporting to him.

Lawrence shook his head in amazement. "I tell ya, Cal, I'm callin' it now. By this time next year, he and Ally will have tied the knot."

"You think so?"

"Yep. That woman and kiddo have roped our brother in, for sure."

"Well, you and Ruby should be getting close to tying the knot too, right? I mean, you did ask her to marry you already."

"That I did." Lawrence grinned. "But she's all frettin' about when to set the date. I told her I'd marry her tomorrow, but she wants it to be 'just right,' so until she sets a date, I'm just waitin' for my cue. How about you and Al? You plan on sealin' that deal soon?"

"When she's ready," Calvin said. "She's getting there, but Alice can't be rushed into anything, and when she does commit to something, you have to make her think it's her idea."

"You already have the ring, don't you?"

Calvin fished into his front pant pocket. "I carry it with me every day just waiting on her to pop the question."

Lawrence laughed. "It'll happen before ya know it."

Calvin grunted and nudged the ring back into his pocket. "I've got to get back on the skid steer." He slapped Lawrence on the back and jogged back to his equipment, Lawrence tossing a wave towards Hayes before climbing into his own truck and heading back towards his own house. Clint tossed him a wave out the back window of Graham's truck as they drove towards the cow pens, Warden Keller sitting stoically beside him as if his very presence made her uncomfortable. Lawrence chuckled as Clint shot him a thumbs up and a chummy grin.

H

Chapter Four

"You know what's more exciting than cow pens?" Clint's voice tickled her ear as he whispered under his breath while Graham explained their new pen system to Tom. She looked up at him, shielding the sun from her eyes with her hand and waiting for him to continue. "Hunting," he stated.

"And why is that?" she asked.

"Because cows do the same thing every day. It's routine. They graze, you rotate them, you work them in the pens, they go back out to graze, and repeat. With hunting, you never know what will happen. You can track a deer or elk for weeks and when the big hunting day arrives, you may find an even bigger prospect that comes into your view or nothing at all. You never know what you're going to get."

"More risk?" Bailey asked.

"Yeah." Clint smiled. "And there's nothing more exciting than when you have a big bull or buck walk into your line of sight." He looked down at her. "You hunt?"

"I have in the past."

She could tell her comment pleased him by the genuine smile and light that hit his blue eyes. She indulged for a moment, liking the way they lightened to a brighter shade of blue when he was happy about something. He did have a pretty gaze. Rocks crunching under boots had her snapping her attention back to Graham and Tom as they slipped through one of the gates nearest the truck and stood talking a moment more, Graham pointing out various other changes.

"Can I ask you something?"

She looked up at Clint again and nodded.

"You said the other day that there were some regulations I'd need to follow for my hunting operation. I've looked into what all I think I would need, but would you care to share what you know too. That way I can just make sure my bases are covered?"

Bailey fell into step beside him as he tilted his head for her to walk with him. They took the route around the cow pens opposite Graham and

Tom. The wind picked up and a nice breeze felt soft and welcoming against her skin as she mentally ran through a reply for his question. "Well, if you're going to have hunters out here then you will need to get a hunting lease license. This will allow you to release hunting rights on the property to another person. This works with leasers or individual hunters, so it would cover all aspects of your commercial operation."

"Mike had mentioned that as well. I'm trying to figure out if Graham would need to sign off on that or if I would suffice."

"I'm assuming you will be separating this operation from the other operations on the ranch?" she asked.

He nodded. "Financially, yes. I want to set it up as its own separate business, essentially."

"Then if you are the manager, it's your name that needs to be on the forms. However, if Graham is the only one who is linked as the manager to whatever you guys do out here, then it would need to be him."

"Hayes runs the horses, and operates separately from the 7H behemoth, so I reckon I can too." Clint rubbed a hand over his chin. "That's my hope, anyway."

"You'll also have to make sure that all your hunters have the proper licensing when they're on the property. Trust me, they could get ticketed if not." She smirked and he nudged her with his elbow. A soft laugh bubbled out of her before she continued. "And if they choose to harvest an animal, the proper tag needs to be attached immediately. Meat needs to be properly secured. You have a freezer on the property?"

"Not yet." Clint motioned for her to follow him. They walked a little way from the main hub of the ranch, and he pointed to an open spot under a couple of trees. "That's where I plan on setting up the cooler and skinning shed. I've got several options drafted up and picked out, I just need to have Graham sign off on one before I can start working on it. Cal's already cleared my spot for me though."

"That'll be good. Definitely want to harvest as much meat as you can. So much goes to waste."

"Man, I noticed that in New Mexico this fall. So much meat was just left. The hunters wanted their trophies and then the guides all divided up the meat, had it processed, and took it home. I think I stocked all the freezers here on the ranch and Philip's freezer, Annie's freezer, and even Doc Wilkenson's. And it was the good stuff, especially the elk meat."

"And do you plan on processing the meat yourself here?"

"Possibly, though we have a decent meat market there in Parks. Grayson does a good job with processing. I've actually thought about partnering with him, allowing him to keep some for the market but then somehow creating a donation weekend of some sort."

"Donation?"

"You know, to families in need or somethin' like that. I mean, meat can be expensive. And if we have a ton of meat that needs a place, might as well let folks have it and utilize it. Keeps it from going to waste and feeds the community."

Impressed, Bailey studied him a moment. He paused. "What?"

She smiled. "I think it's a good idea. A kind one."

"I'm a nice guy," Clint assured her. "Most of the time." He chuckled as she rolled her eyes.

"Well, if you're planning on donating the meat, you will need each hunter to sign a wildlife resource document that basically says they don't want their meat. It's noted on their tag, and then you have the liberty to donate that meat."

"You know, I should have brought a notepad to write all this down so I don't forget." He patted his shirt pocket for a pen that wasn't there, and she handed him her phone. His brow furrowed in confusion.

"Put in your email address and I'll email you the forms you'll need."

He tapped around on her phone and then handed it back. "Thanks."

"No problem." Bailey pointed towards Graham and Tom waiting at Graham's truck. "Looks like our ride is ready to move on."

"We could take my truck around," Clint offered. "I could show you my proposed lease boundaries and—"

"Clint, come on!" Graham yelled. "The wardens don't have all day, and neither do I!"

Bailey watched Clint's back stiffen and his jaw set in frustration. He looked similar to his brother, though she doubted he'd ever admit it or want to even recognize the likeness.

"Sorry, Graham can get a bit bossy."

"Maybe another time, then." Those blue eyes landed on her once again and his lips tilted in a small smile of appreciation.

"Yeah. Another time." He led her back to the truck and opened her door, the gentlemanly gesture surprising but appreciated.

"Going to be a beautiful wedding out here," Tom commented as Clint closed her door and jogged to the other side.

Graham grunted in agreement. "I think I almost lost Julia when I set the pasture ablaze."

Tom and Graham laughed as Graham directed the truck towards the pasture where the grand event would take place.

Clint leaned towards Bailey and pointed out the front windshield. "Julia, Graham's fiancé, 'bout wrung our necks for burnin' the pasture. But now she sees how pretty it is." A green, lush pasture awaited them, the grass fresh, vibrant, and healthy. "Though she might be sad once we start mowin' it, right Graham?"

"It'll look pretty. I've got a plan." His older brother drove back towards the main house and Bailey felt slightly disappointed that their little tour was over. She wanted to see more of the ranch. She also had to admit that she wanted to spend more time with Clint and hear more about his hunting operation plans. She could tell he was excited about it and passionate about it, and she hoped his plans came to fruition. There was a lot of groundwork that needed to be laid if he planned to execute a successful first season.

"Thank you for the tour, Mr. Hastings." Bailey shook Graham's hand.

"Glad you guys came out. Gave me a break from wedding planning." He smirked. "Next week's entire work schedule is prepping the pasture for the big day."

"Much to his disappointment," Clint replied.

"I'm not disappointed to be getting married," Graham defended.

"No, but you are disappointed that mowin' grass, settin' up tents, and creating a venue are pulling you away from your beloved cattle," Clint pointed out. Graham's lips thinned, but he didn't deny the charge. Clint laughed and patted him on the shoulder. "It'll be alright, bro. The ranch will go on. And when you're sittin' on a beach with Julia, sippin' some fruity little drink, we'll be slaving away here for you, so when you come back, it will be just as great as when you left."

"It better be."

Clint winked at Bailey as he tapped the brim of his hat. "I've got to get. I'm helpin' Cal this afternoon before we call it quits for the weekend."

Graham dismissed his brother and Clint offered one last wave towards Bailey as he backed his truck out of his brother's drive. He paused, his gaze holding hers a moment longer as if he wanted to say something else to her, but instead, he gave a final nod of farewell and went on his way. Oddly, disappointment settled in her chest at his departure.

~

A cell phone ring had Clint stifling a heavenward, 'thank you,' as Alice's name blinked across the screen of his cell phone and gave him a reason to pause the push mower he'd been stuck with while Calvin used the riding lawn mower to trim a path in the wedding pasture. Curiosity at why she'd be calling him, especially during bachelorette weekend, had him answering quickly. "Why, Alice Wilkenson, I wasn't sure you even had my number. To what do I owe this great pleasure?"

"Shut up, idiot." Alice's typical snide remark had him laughing.

"What's up, Al?"

"You near Cal?"

"Yep. He's mowing."

"Can you flag him down?"

"What for?" Clint asked.

"Because I need him."

"So you call me?"

"He didn't answer his phone."

"And how did you know to call me?"

"Does it matter?" she barked and then sighed. "Because I called Lawrence, and he told me you were workin' with Cal."

"Gotcha." Clint waved a hand in the air to garner Cal's attention when he turned the next curve of grass. He pointed at his phone when Cal noticed him, and Cal lifted the blades and headed his direction. "He's coming. What's going on? You girls okay?"

"We're fine," Alice replied. "Sort of. Look, we're about to leave the spa and we have a nail salon we're headed to next down the walkway, but after that, we're to drive to this fancy restaurant to eat."

"Yeah..." Clint, confused as to why her tone had hushed to almost a whisper, prodded. "And?"

"And my truck won't start. I ran out there to roll the windows down and I think my battery is dead."

Clint couldn't help the bubble of laughter that rumbled out of his chest. "Of course it is."

"Look, I already feel bad, I don't need you to rub it in. I haven't told the girls yet. I'm hoping I won't have to."

"And you want Cal to come give your truck a jump? That's a bit of a drive. You could just ask someone there."

"I don't want to ruin Julia's weekend. I assured her everything would go smoothly."

Cal walked up, swiping his arm over his forehead. "What's up?"

Clint handed him the phone. "It's your lady."

Concern washed over Calvin's face. "Alice? You alright?" He listened and then his shoulders relaxed. "I see." He looked to Clint and pointed in a scolding manner as Clint began to chuckle at the predictability of Alice having truck troubles. "You know, Clint and I will head that way and take care of it." Cal waited. "I've got it, Al, don't worry. You won't even see us. Alright... love y—" He looked at the phone. "She already hung up." He handed Clint his phone. "Up for a trip to Fort Stockton to replace a truck battery?"

"As long as you buy me dinner."

"Deal." Cal pointed to the mowers. "Let's park these under the hay barn for tomorrow. I don't feel like loadin' them up."

Though he smelled like fresh cut grass and sweat, Clint didn't mind the air-conditioned ride to Fort Stockton with Calvin. He and his brother tended to have good conversations when they were together, and Clint liked that Cal listened. Even though he was the second oldest Hastings brother, Calvin never threw his authoritative weight around. Clint shared what all Warden Keller had told him about the different licenses needed to do what he'd like to do for the hunters and for the meat donation program he intended to set up.

"You ordered a cooler yet?"

"Well, I may not have to. I talked to Philip about reachin' out to other ranches to see if I could find a used one from someone. Cheaper that way. Philip thinks he's got one lined up for me, but I may have to put a new compressor on it."

"I figured you'd want a brand new shiny one." Cal smirked as Clint shook his head.

"Not right now. I've got other costs to consider. I just spent most of my guide tips from this fall on game cameras to set up after the wedding. I need to get a good idea of what we've got, survey basically, and Mike's going to help me draft up a sustainable harvest plan for this year."

Cal turned into the parking lot of a swanky hotel, the resort boasting upscale vehicles, valet drivers, and bellmen at the ready to intercept them. Cal's old Shirley pulling into the parking lot was sure to set them abuzz, Clint thought.

"Looks like that's Al's truck there." Clint pointed across the parking lot and Cal turned his truck into the parking area designated for valet parking only. A valet driver darted after them and met them in the lot. "Do you wish to valet, sir?"

"No." Calvin pointed to Alice's truck. "I'm here to put a new battery in that truck there."

"Sir, you cannot access a vehicle in the valet lot if your name is not tied to the vehicle's registration form."

"Right. Well, let me give my girlfriend a call, and you can sort that out with her." Cal dialed Alice's number and with a significant amount of grumbling, she agreed to walk down to the lot.

She arrived wearing a white, terry cloth robe, her hair wrapped up high in a towel on her head, and her feet bare. "I need him to fix my truck." She told the valet. "Thanks." She waved him off and the man continued standing there. "Look," Alice turned to him. "I'm needing a new battery in my truck. He's here to fix it. It will only take a minute and then he and that monstrosity," She pointed to Cal's truck, "will be gone." The valet disappeared and Alice hugged Cal. "Thank you, thank you, thank you. Have I told you that I love you? I do. I absolutely love you. Thank you." He grinned and gave her a quick kiss. He tugged on the tie of her robe. "I like this."

She swatted his hand away. "I was in the middle of a massage."

"Ooooooh, fancy," Clint chimed, holding the new battery for her truck in his hands.

"It is, actually," Alice replied. "I honestly feel a little out of my element, but the ladies are loving it, and this was Annie's idea, so I'm rolling with it."

"You're a good friend." Cal kissed her again.

"And we're sorry you're suffering," Clint replied sarcastically.

Alice stuck her tongue out at him and then grinned. "Thanks for comin', guys. I owe you."

"I'll make a note of that." Clint checked his finger in the air, and she waved him away.

"Not you. Cal. Okay," She tucked a few loose strands of hair back into her towel turban and straightened her robe. "I've got to get back before they notice I'm gone. You're the best." She squeezed Cal once more and then whispered. "And I missed seeing you." She hurried away, stumbling once when her bare feet stepped on a piece of gravel. They heard her hiss before limping back towards the side door of the hotel. Cal stood with a sloppy grin on his face.

"You've got it bad, bro."

"I do."

"Well, if you can manage to swipe off that lovesick puppy look on your face, we have a battery to replace. She won't be so lovey-dovey if we're still workin' on this thing when they leave the hotel."

"You've got that right." Cal unlocked Alice's truck and popped the hood. "Oh, Al," he shook his head when he saw the corroded battery terminal. "Gotta love her."

H

Chapter Five

"Get that tent up!"

"I get it. He's stressing." Hayes rubbed a tired hand over his face as sweat dripped down his temples and he looked to Clint, Lawrence, and Philip. "But the yelling? Really? I mean, we're helping *him*, not the other way around. He should be grateful we're out in this heat."

"Graham would choose the hottest spring in decades to get married," Philip muttered, the heat even taking its toll on him.

Julia, Alice, Annie, and Ally stood to the side watching the men set polls and secure canvas, fretting over placement and 'centeredness.'

"Be careful," Julia called, as Lawrence's hands slipped and the right corner of the large tent buckled.

"Why didn't we hire someone for this?" Seth asked. "Don't people get paid for this?"

"Julia was all about hiring help, but Graham, Mr. Budget, wouldn't let her," Calvin explained.

"Well, all I can say is that the rest of you better decide to get hitched somewhere else or hire a crew to do this mess when it's your turn." Seth tugged on the rope and hooked it to the ground anchor, falling onto his rear when he finally released the tension of the rope.

Ally walked up and placed a hand on Hayes' shoulder and offered him a bottle of water. He chugged half before tossing it to Seth to finish.

"Must be nice," Cal said. "Having your girl bring you water!" he yelled in Alice's direction, and she took a long, satisfying drink with dramatic flair in response. Annie gave her a small shove his direction and Alice walked over and extended her drink towards him. "Thank you."

"It's coming together," Alice encouraged. "And Julia is loving it."

"That's what matters." Hayes placed his hat back on his head and welcomed Annie with a smile when she walked up with her hands on her hips.

"You boys make this woman proud, all comin' together to help Graham and Julia for their big day. I can't believe it's in two days." She placed a hand over her lips as her voice cracked with emotion. She waved away all the boys as they all took a step towards her. "No, no, no. Go away." Though she allowed Hayes to swoop her into a tight hug. "You know you boys mean so much to me. I just love seein' Graham so happy." They all looked Graham's direction as he angrily kicked the dirt and tossed his hat on the ground in response to Lawrence losing one of the rope anchors. They laughed.

"So happy." Philip grinned as Annie watched Julia place a calming hand on his arm and Graham instantly stilled.

"She has a way with him that none of us do, and that's how you know it's special." Annie dabbed at the corners of her eyes again. "All of you have just been so blessed with wonderful women."

"Not all of us," Seth chimed in, motioning to himself and Clint.

"You will be," Annie assured him. "But the rest of you, if your momma and daddy could see all of you so happy and settled, I tell you... they'd burst with happiness. Henry and I are so thankful to share in your joy."

"Annie, we wouldn't be who, what, and where we are without you and Henry, so we are the ones who are thankful." Hayes squeezed her shoulders and then muttered an 'uh oh' as he saw the Texas Game Warden vehicle pull up near the tent location. "Who's in trouble?" He looked at Clint as Warden Keller climbed out of her truck, a folder in her hands, and her steps purposeful.

Annie whacked Clint on the arm. "What did you do now?"

Baffled, Clint shrugged. "Nothing. That I know of."

Bailey walked up with a friendly smile and nodded towards everyone. Her focus, though shielded by sunglasses, landed on Clint. "Nice touch, not keying in your email address into my phone."

His lips tilted into a grin that had her pulse kick up a notch.

"Like'd that, did you?"

She lifted her glasses and tucked them on top of her head. "Sure, Mr. Hastings."

"It's Clint. I thought I established that." He nodded to the phone strapped to the belt on her hip.

"Right. Well, if you have a minute." She nodded over her shoulder for him to follow her and he did, gently placing a hand at the small of her back as he escorted her towards her truck.

"What on Earth is he up to?" Annie asked.

"I think he likes the new warden." Seth stood to his feet, and they all watched as Bailey handed Clint the folder she'd brought.

"She is pretty," Annie added.

"And blonde," Alice continued, receiving a weird look from Cal. "What?" she asked. "Clint usually goes for blondes. It was just an observation."

"I think her hair looks more red." Hayes tilted his head and looked to Ally. "You're the hairdresser, what would you call it?"

Ally tapped her chin. "Strawberry blonde."

"Strawberry? That what we're calling the new warden?" Lawrence walked up and grinned. "I like it. Hey, Strawberry!" he called before taking a thump to the back of the head from Philip.

"You're such a fool. We were talkin' about her hair color."

"Oh." Lawrence joined the group that stared as Bailey and Clint continued talking.

"I apologize for the audience." Clint, without even looking over his shoulder, flipped through the folder. "I figured they were all staring."

She chuckled. "You would be right. Should I handcuff you for kicks?"

KATHARINE E. HAMILTON

His eyes darted up to her face and he laughed, deep and hearty, at her suggestion before tapping her on the head with the folder. "Not with Annie here. Joke or not, she'd find a switch and spank me."

"Now that would be something to see." She leaned to the side to look Annie up and down. "She's small, but I'd put money on her."

"Aren't you full of jokes today." Clint held up the folder. "Thanks for these. I wasn't sure if you'd find my note in your phone or not."

"I figured you'd put your email address in the notes app. I wasn't expecting the message to "bring them to you". I almost didn't. On principle."

"What principle?"

"I didn't want you to think you could boss me around." Bailey crossed her arms, leaned her wait to the back of her feet, and rocked back and forth.

"Did you ever think that I wasn't trying to be bossy? That maybe it was an excuse for me to see you again?"

She froze in her rocking and looked up at him.

"I like your eyes, by the way." He pointed towards her face. "They're a pretty green color right now. The other day they looked more blue."

He was commenting on her eyes? Bailey, mystified, looked at the folder in his hands to hide the flush she felt staining her cheeks.

"Don't be embarrassed, Warden Keller." He tapped the folder against his palm. "I won't let my attraction for you get in the way of your job."

"Wait, your—" She paused, trying to let his comment sink in before responding. "I'm sorry, I'm just here to deliver the license paperwork for you."

"I know. And I appreciate it. But I still think you're cute. Can I say that?" Clint asked.

"Um—"

"Clint, stop harassing the warden." Graham walked forward and offered his hand. "Warden Keller. What brings you out?"

She pointed to the folder in Clint's hands. "Just some documents for Clint to look over for his hunting operation."

"Laws? Regulations? Rules?" Seth followed his big brother and stood on the other side of Clint. "You realize which brother you're giving those to, right?"

Clint shoved his younger brother to the side. "Give it up, Seth. It's information we need for the operation."

Bailey's eyes surveyed the white tent. "Looks beautiful."

Graham sighed. "It's not centered, but I don't have it in me to move it."

"You can't even tell from here." She pointed towards a cluster of trees and the fence line. "What are you basing it off of? Because it's centered perfectly between those trees and the property line."

Graham stepped forward and turned, standing next to her and viewing the scene from her standpoint. "I think you're right." His voice held relief.

"We'll just say that was the plan all along." Clint smiled in thanks to Bailey.

"Oh, hi there, Warden Keller!" Annie waved enthusiastically as she hurried over, grabbing Bailey into a tight hug. "I'm so glad you came out to see us." She pulled back, her eyes full of warmth and welcome. "Ally was right, a perfect and pretty strawberry blonde." She touched the tips of Bailey's hair and smiled at Graham. "We were tryin' to figure it out."

"Oh." Bailey lifted a nervous hand, not used to having people compliment her hair or her eyes.

"Annie, don't embarrass her." Clint flashed an apologetic glance towards Bailey, and she felt her hand being tugged out of the group of men and Annie leading her towards the other women.

"While you're here, you might as well give some female advice. We were discussin' some wedding details and need a tie breaker," Annie explained. She waved Julia down and motioned to Bailey. "An unbiased perspective, Julia."

"Oh. Bailey, right?" Julia asked.

"Yes." Bailey offered a shy smile.

"Wonderful." Julia spread her arms out to encompass the entire space beneath the massive tent. "I'm struggling with where to put the dance floor. Alice and Annie think it should be on this side." She motioned to the left of the tent. "Ally and I think it should be over here, and tables on that side. What do you think?"

Bailey took a step back, taking in the space under the tent but also the setting sun coming over the horizon. "What about the middle?" She tugged Julia to where she stood and pointed to the sun. You would line up perfectly with the sunset, which would make for pretty photos. Well, if your wedding is in the evening."

"It is." Julia's voice trailed off as she surveyed the image Bailey had painted. "And I like it. The middle it is." She turned to the other women, and they all nodded. "Thanks."

"No problem. It's going to be a beautiful set-up."

"I hope so." Julia nervously wound her hands together.

"Honey, it's going to be phenomenal. Your momma carried on all last night about it at the house."

"Where is your mom, actually?" Alice looked around and realized they'd been missing her all along.

"I sent her for a day of pampering. Actually, I forced my dad to take her for a day of pampering." Julia shrugged her shoulders as if guilty of a heinous crime. "She was... starting to overwhelm me."

Alice laughed. "I can only imagine. Need Bailey to cuff her?"

"Alice," Annie scolded. "No one is to wear handcuffs unless it's Julia on her honeymoon."

Julia's jaw dropped as well as Ally's as Alice's eyes widened. "Annie! I can't believe you just said that!" Alice hooted in laughter as she pointed to Julia's blushing face.

"What's going on over here?" Graham asked, walking up and sliding a hand around Julia's waist, which made his future bride jump out of her skin. This only encouraged the other women's laughter even more.

Bailey giggled along with them as Graham looked from one face to the other. "Clearly I missed something."

"Yes, honey, you did, and for the better." Annie winked at Julia before she shooed the other women away from the couple.

"Now, Bailey, I'm so glad you stopped by today." Annie patted her arm. "A pretty day for a ride around."

"Oh, well, I just brought Clint some paperwork we discussed the other day. I am headed back to Sanderson this evening."

"Oh, no you're not." Annie waved her hand. "Not until you've had some supper. I've had a pork butt roasting all day, and we're going to have some pulled pork sandwiches, fresh sweet potato fries, and chocolate pie for dessert. And you're invited."

"Wow!" Bailey's taste buds did feel tempted, but she hadn't meant to stay as long as she did. And she didn't know the Hastings family well enough for them or her to feel comfortable crashing a family supper. Especially one that was just a couple of days away from a wedding. "It's sweet of you to offer, but I—"

"Would love to," Clint interrupted. "Great. I'll ride with you up to the house." He grinned as she turned in surprise at his presence.

Annie nodded in approval. "Take her on a walkabout, Clint. That'll give me time to get the table set. Alice, you'll help me."

"And what about me?" Ally asked.

"I thought you had to pick up Ava?" Annie asked.

She shook her head. "No ma'am. My mother is watching her until the wedding so I can help around here."

"Oh, we'll miss that little lady runnin' around wreaking havoc the next couple days." Annie motioned towards Alice's truck. "But I will accept the extra hands for supper prep."

"I can help too," Bailey offered.

"Oh no, honey." Annie waved her away. "You head on up with Clint. We've got this covered."

Bailey, feeling somewhat cornered, turned to find Clint already halfway in her truck, resting an arm on the open passenger door as he leaned against it. "Well, I guess it's just you and me, Warden." He tapped the brim of his hat with a satisfied smile. "You gonna give me a ride?"

Bailey hopped into her truck and Clint chuckled as she turned the key. "What's so funny?"

"I don't think I've ever seen someone sit so close to a steering wheel before."

"Are you calling me short?"

He grinned. "Maybe."

"I'll have you know that I am a solid 5'3", thank you very much."

"Wow, a solid 5'3"? You don't say?"

"Yes." She shifted into reverse and twisted to look out the back window, her hand resting on the back of his seat as she did so. When she adjusted to turn back to the front, she caught the amused gleam in his eyes. "Stop it."

He laughed. "What? I didn't even say anything."

"You didn't have to. I see it on your face." She smirked as she shifted into drive and followed Alice's truck towards Graham's house. "You want to tease me some more."

"True. Very true. But I'm not, so that should count for something."

"Oh, are we keeping points for good behavior now? Because you're in last place."

"Ouch, Warden. That hurts my feelings." He grinned. I happen to know this one time you handcuffed an innocent man for absolutely no reason."

"No reason? Really? You were in my face," she reminded him.

"I tripped."

"And you were yelling."

"I was simply carryin' on a conversation."

"And you were obnoxious."

"I was… trying to get my point across."

She guffawed in surprise laughter. "And what point was that? The 'I'm a Hastings, hear me roar' point?'"

Clint choked on another laugh before his face sobered. "I, uh, yeah, I could see how that would be obnoxious."

"You don't say?" Bailey's brows lifted in mock wonder.

"Alright now, don't get carried away. I apologized, and we agreed to a blank slate, remember?"

"That we did. And so far you've been…"

"I've been…" He encouraged her to continue.

"Tolerable."

"I'll take it." He flashed a devastatingly handsome smile as they pulled up to Graham's house. "Now come on, Annie wants me to give you the tour of the creek."

"Why the creek?" Bailey asked.

"Because she likes you," Clint muttered, and she saw the slight tinge of pink color his ears as they rounded the house.

H

Chapter Six

A loud clap pounded on his back as Henry greeted Clint with a hearty hello. "You boys look polished and pristine. What's the occasion?" He laughed at his own joke as a nervous groom walked down the stairs, trying to button the cuffs of his sleeves. "You alright there, Graham?"

Graham paused three steps from the bottom, almost tripping over his own feet as he looked up. He stumbled, and Clint grabbed him with a steadying hand before he could completely fall. He nodded his thanks. "I'm fine."

"You don't seem fine," Lawrence heckled. "You seem a little jumpy."

"I'm not."

"It's alright if you are." Henry reached up and straightened Graham's boutonniere. "I remember my wedding day like it was yesterday. Annie looked so pretty. My hands shook the entire day, even after the ceremony."

"They did?" Graham asked, his face reflecting the pre-wedding jitters he'd been hesitant to admit to.

Henry chuckled. "You betcha. Don't let your nerves get the best of ya. I promise it's all worth it."

"Don't worry, Graham. If you decide to back out at the last minute, one of us will just fill the position," Clint offered with a wink and Seth raised his hand to volunteer.

"I don't think so." A smile lifted the corner of Graham's mouth as he relaxed a smidgen. "Anyone seen Julia yet?"

Calvin walked in the back door and removed his hat. "Just saw her. She hasn't run yet."

"That's good." Even more relief sounded in Graham's voice.

"You mean she's all dressed and ready?" Lawrence stood. "What are we doing in here, then? Come on boys, let's go take a peek."

Henry laughed as all the brothers scurried out of the house leaving Graham to pace on his own.

Clint stopped in his tracks when Alice opened the door to the guesthouse and a beautiful woman he didn't know stood next to her. "They're here," Alice called over her shoulder.

"Julia was right. Not a bad looking one in the bunch." The stranger smiled and offered her hand to Clint who stood in front. "I'm Caroline Walsh, Julia's friend from New Mexico. Which one of you is Clint?"

"That'd be me." Clint held a hand to his chest, his other hand still holding hers.

"You have the luxury of escorting me down the aisle. Sorry I didn't make rehearsal last night." Caroline stepped aside as Ruby walked out.

"Ruby Cole," Lawrence removed his hat and placed it over his heart. "I think I just fell even more in love with you. Look at you." He spun Ruby in a small spin before leaning in for a light kiss so as not to mess up her lipstick. "You're gorgeous."

"You don't look so bad yourself." Ruby softly touched the tips of his shaggy hair that'd been combed and styled away from his face.

"Helena in there?" Philip asked, eager to see his own girl.

"I'm coming!" Helena called. "Getting a touch up from Ally."

Annie stepped out the door. "Boys, boys, boys. It is not time for the girls to leave yet. Y'all are supposed to go to the wedding site first."

"We couldn't help ourselves, Annie. Cal came in talking about how pretty Jewels looked, so we had to come and see," Clint explained.

Julia's mother, Pam, stepped out and enveloped Clint in a hug. "Don't you look handsome, Clint. Oh, and Lawrence." She hugged the next in line and then the next, offering a compliment to each of them. "How's Graham?"

"Nervous."

"Oh, bless his heart." Pam covered her smile with her fingertips. "Julia is too, but in a good way," she assured them.

A long golf cart arrived out front, a man in a black suit standing and waiting patiently out front. "That's my ride," Pam pointed. "Rodney is already at the wedding site waiting on me. Anyone else need a ride?"

"Are we to ride with Graham?" Seth asked.

All the brothers shrugged.

"The planner should have told you," Alice told them.

"We haven't seen the planner," Hayes reported. "We just got dressed and came over here."

Alice shook her head and rolled her eyes. "Y'all ride with Graham, we ride with Julia. Graham is not to see her before the walk down the aisle. Y'all go first. Then we go."

"See, who needs the planner?" Calvin kissed Alice's cheek. "You look good, Doc."

"I'm going over to see my boy." Annie parted her way through the brothers and headed towards Graham's house as he stepped out onto the porch, placing his cowboy hat on his head.

Annie stopped in her tracks, her hands coming to her mouth as she watched him descend the steps. Her shoulders started to shake, and Graham paused to wrap his arms around her, her small frame disappearing within his hug.

"Welp, Annie's already cryin'." Lawrence smirked, all of them growing glassy-eyed at the sight of their beloved Annie overcome with emotion.

They all walked over to them and wrapped their arms around both her and Graham, a giant Hastings group hug that even encompassed Henry when he stepped out of the house.

"My boys, my boys, my boys." Annie dabbed a tissue under her eyes when they all stepped away. "Your parents would be so happy to see this day. All of you here. And Graham, honey," She hugged him one more time. "you're a good boy. You are, sweetie. I'm so proud of you." She patted him on the back once more and then inhaled a deep breath. "Alright, that's enough blubbering. Ally worked hard to make me look like a knock-out, I can't let my mascara run." Annie linked her arm with Henry's. "Let's get to that wedding."

Half of the brothers loaded up on one cart as the others followed in another. Guests had been arriving for the last half hour and found their seats in the white chairs the brothers set up the day before. The wedding would take place in the middle of the pasture, behind the reception tent, so that the horizon was the backdrop for the nuptials. All Julia had wanted were white chairs, an aisle runner, and flowers. Nothing more. Nothing fancy. Simple. The ranch was her decoration, and it was showing off with beautiful weather, green grass, and a slight breeze. Clint would even admit to saying an extra prayer or two that morning in hopes the day would be perfect for Graham and Julia.

As he watched his brothers pair off with their women, he felt a new sense of longing for what he saw in their faces. Companionship, friendship, and in some instances, love. He'd seen them all smitten for months, but as Clint watched Lawrence tuck Ruby's hair behind her ear, and Philip whisper something to Helena that made her smile, and Calvin press his lips to Alice's forehead, Clint realized he wanted that too. He wanted someone to dote upon, to kiss, to caress, to whisper sweet things to. He wanted someone who not only tolerated him but needed him. Needed his presence in their lives in order to feel centered. His brothers had found that. Was it crazy for him to want it too? He'd admit that he wasn't exactly the settling down type, but what if he'd changed? What if what he wanted was to run a successful hunting operation on the 7H, live in the house he'd worked so hard to build, and have a wife and family to come home to? Bailey's face came to mind, their walk around the creek before supper a couple of nights ago replaying in his mind. He'd learned more about the cute warden, that she was an outdoorsy gal who turned her love into her work, much like he was trying to do. And she'd listened even more to his plans for the hunting season. How he intended to utilize his house as a bunkhouse. How Annie'd already agreed to cook for the hunters, and how Seth would help guide. Logistics that most people found boring or tuned out when he started talking about them, but Bailey hadn't. She asked questions, helped sort out details, and encouraged him, which was new. He'd had few who actually encouraged him. If he'd been smart, he would have asked her to be his plus one to the wedding, but intellect wasn't his strong suit when it came to women.

"You alright?" Alice placed a hand on Clint's arm as she lined up next to Hayes for the procession down the aisle.

"Yes ma'am." He smiled. "Just thinkin'."

"Weddings will do that to you." She grinned as Hayes' attention came back to her after chatting with Philip.

"What'd I miss?"

"Nothing." Clint smirked. "I'm just soaking in all the festivities, the beautiful women, and the moment."

"My beautiful women are right up there." Hayes waved towards an excited Ava and Ally who sat behind Annie and Henry up at the front.

"Calvin's made me a bit weak-kneed," Alice admitted, smiling up at Cal as he stood next to Graham at the end of the aisle. "But don't tell him I said that."

Clint laughed. "You're next, Al. You and Cal will be making the same walk here soon."

"He hasn't even asked me to marry him yet," Alice whispered. "so it may be a while."

"Ya never know." Hayes squeezed her hand and winked at Clint.

Caroline walked up next to him and linked her arm with his. "Sorry, I was chatting with my sister-in-law, Rory. She just got here." She pointed to a black and purple-haired woman sitting at the end of a row. "My husband doesn't really do social events, so Rory came instead. They both love Julia. You have a girl here?"

"No."

"Really?" Her brows lifted. "I'm surprised."

"Why's that?" Clint asked curiously.

Caroline flashed a warm smile. "All you handsome cowboys... I figured you boys had the girls lined up."

He scoffed as Hayes shoved him from behind to take a step forward.

"Not exactly."

The music started and Clint led Caroline down the aisle before splitting to their respective sides as one by one the groomsmen and bridesmaids found their place. The music shifted to 'Canon in D' and Julia stood at the back of the aisle with her father, Rodney. The attendees stood, and Clint watched as Graham looked up the aisle.

Julia's lips split into a nervous but radiant smile and Graham... Clint watched as Calvin placed a firm hand on his brother's shoulder to keep him steady. Graham's nerves and love were written all over his face as Julia grew closer.

A breeze ruffled her dress and veil, adding to her whimsical appearance, and Clint watched Graham take two solid deep breaths as if he were trying to refrain from sprinting towards her instead of waiting patiently for her arrival. When the moment came for Rodney to give her hand to

Graham, Graham lunged at the man, lifting him an inch off the ground in a firm hug. Rodney chuckled and patted his back, giving Graham's shoulder a squeeze before kissing his daughter's cheek and finding his place in his seat next to Pam. Graham lifted Julia's hand to his lips and kissed it before nodding towards the pastor to get on with the ceremony. Julia, with stars in her eyes, stared lovingly up at Graham.

Clint's heart pounded in his chest. This was Graham. His hard, stubborn, unfriendly, grumpy older brother lost absolutely in love. He couldn't recall ever seeing Graham smile so much, and the world seemed to have lifted off his brother's shoulders and vanished into thin air. He was lighter, happier, joyful even, and Clint stared in complete awe of the transformation.

"You may now, kiss your bride," the pastor announced, Clint realizing he'd zoned out through the vows. He watched as Graham lightly and chastely kissed Julia's lips, but Julia wasn't having it. When Graham started to pull away and turn towards the crowd, Julia tugged on the lapels of his vest and placed a passionate and thorough kiss on his lips, leaving the crowd in cheers, whistles, and excitement. Her face blushed when she released him, and Graham's chummy smile spoke volumes of his love for her.

"Ladies and gentlemen," the pastor announced. "Mr. and Mrs. Graham Hastings."

More cheers erupted as they walked down the aisle, hand in hand, to a lively tune provided by the string quartet. Clint offered his arm to Caroline, and they followed the rest of the couples back down the aisle and towards a separate tent that allowed the wedding party to have a moment before the start of the reception.

Clint walked up to Julia and lifted her off her feet, spinning her in a small circle. She giggled as he kissed her cheek. "You're stuck with us all now, Jewels."

Her eyes found Graham's, "I wouldn't have it any other way."

"You say that now," Alice warned, stepping to the side as Ally and Ava ducked into the tent and Ally began work at touching up Julia's makeup for her reception entrance.

Ava slid her hand into Graham's, his older brother startling a moment before kneeling down next to her. "Hi there, Ms. Ava. You sure look pretty."

"I knew you were a prince." Ava kissed his cheek before running shyly back towards Hayes, who lifted her into the air on a toss and settled her on his hip.

Lawrence swiped his pocket square over his eyes and Julia hugged him. "I get emotional at these sorts of things, Jewels, I apologize. But you look so good, and Graham looks so happy."

Graham slapped him on the back in a laugh.

"Stop blubberin'." Alice shook her head in dismay as she reached over and squeezed Julia's hand. "I'm happy you're forever stuck with me too."

Before they could all fully catch their breath, the photographer, a different one than Julia had used for her bridals, walked into the tent to hurry them through wedding photos while the sun was right. A blur, Clint thought. All of it was one big, happy and joyous blur.

~

Bailey flicked the channel for the hundredth time, her television either boasting bachelors handing out roses, a hospital drama, or a crime show. She wasn't in the mood for any of them. She didn't watch much television, but tonight she needed noise. She wanted the company. Typically, she didn't mind the quiet of her apartment, but the sounds from the small bar down the street had her wishing she'd had Saturday night plans. She stood, sliding her blanket to the side and walked towards the small kitchenette and looked in her refrigerator. Sighing, she grabbed a container of onion dip and reached for the bag of potato chips on the counter. A little late-night snack might help keep her entertained for a bit as she channel surfed. Her cell phone buzzed, and she glanced at the clock. Eleven. *Who would be texting so late?*

She grabbed her phone off the kitchen counter and walked it over to the couch with her dip and chips. Opening the messages app, she saw Clint Hastings' number in her inbox: *"You up?"*

"Interesting," Bailey muttered, sending a hasty response.

Bailey: *"Yes. Everything okay?"*

Clint: *"Perfect."*

A picture of Graham and Julia dancing in the middle of the dance floor popped up on her screen.

Bailey*: "Beautiful."*

Clint: *"I should have asked you to be my plus one for tonight."*

Bailey: *"Why's that?"*

Clint: *"So you could see this. I have to admit, it's been an incredible wedding. I've never seen Graham like this before."*

Bailey*: "Congratulations to him and Julia."*

Bailey waited for another text, but Clint had left the conversation, no doubt enjoying the festivities. Disappointment had her flicking through channels on her television again. *Why was she looking forward to a text from Clint Hastings of all people?* Her phone dinged with an incoming message, and she snatched it off the end table.

Clint: *"Have a good night, Warden."*

Bailey: *"You could just call me Bailey, like a normal person."*

Clint: *"Now where's the fun in that?"*

She grinned, her fingers hesitating over her phone before she started texting back.

Bailey: *"Good night, Mr. Hastings."*

Clint: *"Fine. I'll call you Bailey if you promise not to call me Mr. Hastings."*

Bailey: *"Deal."*

No other text came through. She couldn't blame him for soaking up time with his family and enjoying seeing his brother so happy. Family weddings were meant to be enjoyed by everyone. But what if he had asked her to be his plus one? Would she have said yes? *No.* She knew she wouldn't have, which was unfortunate, because right now, she wanted to be there. With Clint. Of all people, the arrogant, smug, and confident Clint Hastings had wiggled his way into her thoughts and good graces. She couldn't let her attraction towards him keep her from focusing on what was most important: her job. She'd worked hard to be where she was, and she didn't want to distract herself with a handsome face. Especially a handsome face notorious for breaking hearts.

She flicked the channel, the overly made-up bachelor handing a single red rose to an equally made over woman who cried at his attention. She cried, and Bailey cringed. No, she wouldn't be like some frilly rose collector. She didn't need a gorgeous bachelor giving her roses or attention to be happy. And she certainly didn't need it to be Clint Hastings.

7

Chapter Seven

"I see one!" Ava darted through the grass at lightning speed, her little legs barely able to hike through the thick foliage. She reached down and grabbed a deer antler, holding it up with a triumphant cheer.

"Nice one!" Clint reached for it to check it over and handed it back to her.

"Look, Hay! I got one!" She ran over to her mother and Hayes, both giving appreciative sounds. "I'm good at this."

"You are, aren't you?" Hayes asked. "I always loved hunting sheds on the ranch too. But as good as I was, I wasn't as good as Clint. He always knew where to find the best and biggest ones." Hayes nodded towards his brother and Ava, with another Hastings brother in sight to shower with heroic admiration, ran up next to Clint and grabbed his hand. "Let's find more! A big one!"

Clint laughed, picking her up and resting her over his shoulders so she could sit and see at a distance. "This whole pasture should have some good ones. You know why?"

"Nope." Ava rested her hands on top of the worn ballcap he'd slung on that morning as she balanced herself.

"That." He pointed to a pond. "Deer love to be near water. And sometimes when they come to get a drink their antlers will fall off when they bend down."

"They just fall off out of nowhere?" Ally asked curiously as she and Hayes caught up with them.

"No. They're already pretty loose by that point. But you will typically find more near water because that's where they hang out."

"Can't blame them for that." Hayes swiped a shirt sleeve over his sweaty face. "I could go for some cold water about now too."

"I see one! I see one!" Ava wiggled on top of his shoulders and Clint held her ankles tight as he walked in the direction she was pointing. Sure enough, she spotted a prize.

Clint whistled in approval as he lifted her over his head and walked towards the shed. Ava squealed with delight. "Is it a good one? It's real big." She attempted to heft the trophy shed horn and grunted with the effort.

"Ms. Ava you just found an awesome horn."

She echoed his praise in a yell towards Hayes and Ally as they continued searching the grass for more sheds. They flashed smiles and thumbs in her direction.

"See here." He grabbed the shed and held it in his hands. "It's got a real nice and long main beam, good mass," He hefted the horn as if it were a dumbbell which brought forth a giggle from Ava. "and deep forks front and back." He ran his fingers over the horn and then let her do the same. "This would be from a mature mule deer. And it's exactly something I was hoping to find. Good job, Ava."

"I found the winner!" Ava held up her hands and twirled in a circle, her bedazzled jeans and belt glistening in the sunshine.

"Don't celebrate too soon," Clint teased. "We have to find the other one."

"Another one?" she looked up in confusion.

"Well, yeah." Clint shrugged. "Have you ever seen a deer with only one horn?"

Her eyes lit up. "There's unicorn deer?" she danced in glee.

"Whoa, whoa, whoa." Clint laughed. "No. That's not what I meant. I meant there are no deer with only one antler, so that means there's another big one hiding out here."

She stopped her jig and fisted her hands on her hips. "So there are no unicorn deer?"

"No, ma'am. Sorry."

She huffed. "Well, that's just bad. I wanted to see one."

"It would be pretty cool, huh?"

She looked up at an approaching Hayes and squinted against the sun. "Did you know there's no unicorn deer, Hay?"

Hayes's brows lifted. "You don't say. Well, that is just disappointing."

"I know. I said the same thing," Ava replied, her tone a mirror of her mother's, which made both men smile. "Guess I'll have to find the other big one instead." She walked off in the direction of her mother muttering under her breath about the lack of unicorns on the ranch, making Hayes chuckling.

"She's somethin'." Clint grinned at his brother.

Hayes nodded proudly as he watched the two newest women in his life hunt for sheds, their clasped hands slowing Ally's pace, but painting a pretty picture against the backdrop of the ranch.

"And you're lost. Those two roped you in, didn't they?"

Hayes turned his attention back to Clint. "Hm?"

Laughing, Clint handed him the monster-sized shed Ava had found. "Yep. Roped."

Hayes walked with him back towards the truck and placed the shed in the bed. "Can't help it. Wasn't planning on feeling this way about anybody anytime soon, but I guess the good Lord had other plans."

"And when are you popping the question?" Clint asked.

Hayes's face drained of color at the idea. "Oh—" He kicked the dirt on the ground with his boot and avoided Clint's gaze.

"You already have a ring?"

Hayes shook his head. "No, no, nothing like that. Ally needs more time. She's been through a lot. I don't want to rush things. And I want to make sure Ava would be happy too. Ya know?"

"I'd say she's happy." Clint pointed to the little girl as she twirled in circles, her head back, eyes closed, spinning as fast as she could until she stumbled. She then lay in the grass staring up at the clouds.

"Right. Well, we'll see when the timing is right."

"Speaking of timing, have you noticed Graham's been late to the morning meet up pretty much every morning for the last month and a half?" Clint asked.

"Um, he is newly married. So what if he takes a little longer getting out of the house in the mornings?" Hayes smiled. "I imagine it's hard to leave your new and beautiful wife each mornin' after you've been spoiled basking in the sun together in Costa Rica for two weeks and then trying to figure a new routine out at the house."

"True. But he'd have our hide if we were late," Clint pointed out. "Just find it amusing he's now dragging behind in the mornings. And I won't be takin' any hits from him about my time management until he gets his own straightened out."

Hayes, indifferent, shrugged his shoulders. "I just disappear into my stables. I don't care what happens elsewhere or *when*."

"I'm hoping to be like that soon." Clint nodded towards the sheds. "I can't wait to get hunts lined up for this season. Philip helped me find a cooler. Cal's helping me level out the spot for it. Seth and I are going to pour the cement this coming week. Law's got his hat in the ring too, if we need him. Helena already said her dad and brother want to come out again. Last year just gave them a small taste of what the ranch has to offer." He smiled, eager to skip right over summer and straight into fall. "I think it might all actually come together."

Hayes clapped him on the back. "I hope it does for you, Clint. It's important to work your passion. You've always loved hunting. If anyone can kick this off, it's you."

"Really? You think so?"

"I do."

"Well, thanks." Clint's chest warmed at Hayes's confidence in him. It wasn't every day he received praise from any of his brothers. Granted, if he were being honest, he had never really done anything worthy of it. Yet. That was about to change. His goal was to show Graham and the rest of his brothers that his plan to start a hunting operation wasn't hair-brained or half-cocked. It was smart, well-planned, and beneficial, not only to the ranch but the community as well. Big steps, he knew, but he was ready to take them.

They walked down the back property line, searching for more sheds when Hayes held up his hand for everyone to stop. He pointed up ahead and Clint's heart kicked into a happy dance that rivaled Ava's.

"What?" Ally whispered. "What is it?" Already tugging Ava and herself behind Hayes as if a critter were about to get them.

"A wallow." Clint's eyes danced as he smiled. "That ain't no mule deer wallow." He surveyed the ground and knelt to run his fingers over fresh tracks. "Brother, I think we've got ourselves some elk after all."

Hayes knelt beside him and studied the imprinted hoof prints in the ground. "Could be the cows."

"No." Clint pointed to the curve of the shape. "Not cow. Definitely elk. Let's see where they went." He and Hayes walked a couple hundred yards until reaching the property fence between the 7H and the Chandlers' ranch next door. "Agh. I want to see where they head. Stay here." He jogged towards his truck and began rummaging through his back seat. He made it back to Hayes and held up a pair of binoculars.

"Well?" Hayes asked. "See any?"

"No. But I think I know where they're at." He handed Hayes the binoculars and waited patiently.

"The ravine?"

"That'd be my guess. There's shade over there. I bet they ventured over here for the water and are holin' up there during the day." Clint grabbed Hayes's shoulder and jerked him back and forth in excited shoves. "We have elk!"

Hayes, laughing, held up his hands. "Hold on, cowboy. They're currently on Chandler's place. I wouldn't get too excited."

"I'm going to set up a few cameras." Clint's mind already began ticking off what he needed to do and the opportunities that came with having elk on the property. "You know what, I'm going to call Chandler and see if he'll let me check them out."

"Call him?" Hayes asked. "Chandler?"

"Yeah. Why not?"

"Well, for starters, he hates us."

"He doesn't even know us," Clint pointed out.

"He doesn't have to. We're Hastings."

"I'm tryin' it." Clint thumbed through his phone and paused. "I don't have his number. You got it?"

Hayes hesitated a moment and Clint's face split into a radiant smile. "You do, don't you? Come on, Hayes. It's worth a shot. We just want to see if we're right."

"Fine." Hayes fished his phone out of his back pocket and rattled off Bob Chandler's number. Clint dialed and tossed a thumbs up towards Hayes when the line started ringing.

~

Bailey appreciated the family history Bob Chandler provided as he walked around his cow pens, explaining their process of working cattle. It wasn't why she was here, but she enjoyed hearing old ranchers share their legacy with her. Every ranch, every piece of land had a history of hard work. Blood, sweat, tears, and lots of life were poured into the land and Bailey loved soaking a smidgen of that up with each step she took. Bob's granddaughter, Charlotte, walked with them. As the sole heir to the ranch, Charlotte, or Charlie as she liked to be called, shared her view on ranch operations as well. She was young, probably early twenties, Bailey figured, but her mind was sharp and her passion for the land and her respect for her grandfather was evident in the way she listened to him talk and share stories she'd no doubt heard a million times before.

Bob reached into his pant pocket and pulled out an old cell phone, the jingle strangled due to a partially busted up speaker. He flipped it open, and instead of holding it to his ear, he held it out in front of his mouth on speakerphone.

"It doesn't work unless it's on speaker," Charlotte whispered and then rolled her eyes with a smile.

Bailey acknowledged the remark with a nod.

"This is Bob."

"Mr. Chandler, howdy. This is Clint Hastings over on the 7H."

Bob's features hardened and his lips tightened. "Which one are you?"

Bailey's brow furrowed at the sharp, unfriendly tone that came from the old man's mouth.

"Well, I'm the second to the end." Clint's voice was friendly, despite Bob's clipped tone.

Bob grunted. "And what do you want?"

Bailey listened intently, also curious as to why Clint would be calling upon the older man.

"Well, sir, I was back in our Arroyo pasture today checkin' on things and stumbled upon a fresh wallow with some elk tracks. I think there's been a bunch of elk in here. Looks like they just crossed over your fence line and are hanging out in a little tree mott down in a ravine. This would be in your southeast corner. Have y'all seen these elk back here? I was going to see if—"

"There ain't no elk in this country. They're all out west," Bob interrupted on a growl.

"Well, Mr. Chandler, I'm pretty sure it's elk. There's tracks all around the wallow."

"Boy, I've been here seventy years, and there's never been elk over here. They don't come this far east."

"But—"

"You're just like the rest of those Hastings. You don't listen. You just stay on your side of the fence, boy." Bob hung up and muttered a curse under his breath as he shoved the phone into his pocket. "Hastings just wanting to see what we've been doing over in that pasture with that equipment."

"Grandpa, you told me just last week you thought you saw elk tracks in that pasture when you were running the dozer." Charlie crossed her arms and narrowed her gaze on him.

"Yeah, but he don't need to know that. Those are *our* elk, on *our* property." Bob looked to Bailey and shook his head. "Don't know if you've met those Hastings boys, but they're just like their daddy and grandpa, worthless."

"Grandpa—"

"Don't grandpa, me. I know that family better than anybody. They're all no good, a bunch of sour apples, and that Graham Hastings is just like his granddaddy. Stubborn as a mule and as untrustworthy as they come."

Bailey didn't mention her opinion. She still didn't know the Hastings well enough to even muster a defense for them, but from what she'd seen from the brothers so far said quite the opposite.

"Sorry." Charlie motioned towards Bailey's truck, and they started walking in its direction and away from her grumpy grandfather. "My grandpa has huge disdain for the Hastings family."

"Why is that?"

"Oh, something about how their granddaddy cheated him out of the land. He's always felt their ranch should have been his. If it were up to Grandpa, he'd own the entire state of Texas."

"I see." Bailey extended her hand. "Well, I appreciate your time today. If you ever have any concerns or need me, please let me know."

"Thanks, Warden Keller." Charlie waved in farewell, and Bailey headed out the front gate. Clint's excitement over the possibility of elk and the confirmation from Charlotte that they too had seen signs of them in this country, meant this year's hunting season was going to be interesting.

H

Chapter Eight

He was right. He knew he **was** right. No matter what Bob Chandler said, the tracks Clint had seen were elk. His game cameras had finally arrived, and he'd spent the last of his hunting tips on buying enough batteries to keep them running for quite a while, so he tied the buckles around the trees surrounding the water troughs, the wallow, and the fence line. He was going to capture what he could as proof.

His phone rang, and he silenced the call. He knew it was Graham, and he knew he was avoiding cattle work. He wasn't meaning to leave his brothers shorthanded, but he had to get the cameras up today. He'd wasted precious weeks waiting for the cameras to come in, but he'd spotted some fresh tracks two days ago that promised the elk were still frequenting his side of the fence.

His phone rang again, only this time it was Lawrence. He silenced the call as he walked back to his truck and began loading batteries into another one of the cameras and programming its settings.

Another phone call. He sighed, pressing the speaker button. "Yeah?"

Cal's voice came over the line. "You avoidin' us?"

"I'm working."

"Really? I don't see you anywhere around here."

"I'm over in Arroyo and have been since this morning."

"Pretty sure the cows are up here at the pens." Cal's irritated tone did nothing to affect Clint's hopeful mood.

"Well, if you're wanting the support of Graham on this whole hunting idea of yours, shirking your regular ranch duties isn't going to do it."

"He'll understand once I tell him we officially have elk on the ranch."

Silence filled the line. "Elk?"

Clint smiled at the trace amount of excitement he heard in Cal's voice. "Yep. Seems Hayes was right when he spotted them a while back. I've got tracks to prove it. I'm setting up cameras now to see if I can get some pictures."

"You don't have any pictures yet?"

"No."

"But tracks?"

"Yep."

"You sure? Could just be cow tracks."

"I'm sure. Trust me."

"Alright. Well, at least try and make it up here for the tail end of things. Graham's not happy you're skippin' out."

"I'll make it up to him. I'll check the troughs while I'm back here and on the way up so as to appease him there."

"Good deal." Cal hung up and Clint carried a metal t-post to a shady spot near the water and began driving it into the ground. When he felt it was secure, he tied the camera up. Two cameras on the wallow, one on the water, he was set.

On his drive towards the front of the ranch, he called Mike. The friendly wildlife biologist answered on the second ring.

"Clint Hastings, what can I do for you?"

"Hey Mike. Got a question for ya."

"Shoot." He heard a pencil tapping against a desk and pictured Mike leaning back in his desk chair with his feet propped up.

"You had any reports of elk coming into this area?"

"Elk?" Mike gave a low whistle. "That'd be a nice little tidbit, wouldn't it? But no, I haven't. Granted, I don't usually receive such reports. I could make a few calls and see what I can find out. You got eyes on some?"

"Well, I believe I've found some tracks on the property. I set up some cameras to see what I can find out."

"I'll get back with you. Keep me updated on those photos though."

"Will do." Clint hung up and pulled up next to Graham's truck, the brothers all gathered around the tailgate, sipping water, and resting from finishing up working cows.

"And the prodigal son returns." Lawrence smirked as Clint stepped out of his truck and shut the door. "You sure look chipper."

"I am." Clint nodded towards Graham. "Sorry for the absence. I was in Arroyo."

"Cal told us," Graham replied, his firm tone relaying his annoyance. But his lack of a lashing told Clint he was more intrigued than upset.

"I'm telling you, we have elk."

Hayes waved his hand as if proving his claims from months ago was finally confirmed.

"Pictures?"

"Not yet," Clint said. "I called Mike and he's going to ask around to see if there are any other reports or sightings. This could be great, Graham. If we have elk on the property, we'll have hunters fighting over a spot to come here."

"We'll see. By the way, Philip is bringing your cooler out Friday. I suggest if you want to place it, you better finish up that slab to put it on."

"It's ready. Just got to run wire over from the house to hook up electricity."

"You sure you want it that close to your house?" Hayes asked.

"Makes sense. I'm going to use my house as the lodge while I stay with Cal."

"You are?" Calvin asked.

"Yep. Thought I told you." Clint grinned.

"Why me?"

"Because you already wake up super early, so I figured it'd be less of a nuisance if I'm banging cabinets at five in the morning on hunting days."

Cal shrugged as if he didn't mind, and Clint continued. "Eventually, maybe we can build a separate bunk house or lodge, but for starters, my house it is."

Graham didn't say a word but removed his hat and swiped the sweat from his forehead before setting it back in place. "Guess you better get to it, then. We're done here for today."

Clint's phone rang and Mike shared that the warden had received reports of elk sightings and tracks coming from the northwest through properties in their area. He knew immediately it was Chandler's place even though the old man had lied over the phone. That was alright. He knew, and he was going to catch them on camera.

Cal walked up and tapped him on the shoulder when he hung up.

"What's up?"

"We've got rain on the radar for this week."

"You want me to do a rain dance?" Clint asked.

"Wouldn't hurt, but what I'm gettin' at is that we will probably be workin' on equipment if the radar proves true."

"Right."

"I'm tied up in the morning with Alice. Could you make a trip to Sheffield and pick up some parts for me?"

"Not a problem."

"I called them in, so they'll be ready for ya."

"Got it." Clint tapped the edge of his hat in salute and hopped in his truck. Sheffield in the morning, rain in the afternoon, and an early quitting time. Clint couldn't wait for tomorrow.

~

She hadn't been on the back roads much in the last few months. She usually avoided them, but the summer months brought lots of fishermen along the creeks, lakes, and rivers. They'd tuck themselves away and she'd drive the winding country roads to check licenses. Illegal dumping had been her last ticket to write. Trash was not meant to be left on the side of the road or at an empty campsite. And now it was late, one in the morning to be exact, and she was exhausted. Her windshield wipers swished across the glass in front of her. The rain, though predicted for later in the morning, had unleashed upon her sooner than expected. The roads were slick, and the rain pounding down and trees tunneling overhead obstructed her view, and when she rounded the curve, her tires lost traction. She tapped the brakes and gripped the steering wheel as her back end slid across the muddy dirt road. She spun her steering wheel to the left to correct course, but misjudged, and sent her truck into a fishtail even worse than before. The momentum and downpour drove her right off the road into the trench. Her head slammed forward, narrowly missing connecting with the steering wheel. Her seatbelt constricted, hugging her to her seat. Her heart pounded as she collected her nerves and reversed her truck to try and back out of the trench and onto the road. Her tires spun and she sank further into the mud. The thud and swish of the windshield wipers kept her company as she struggled with what to do. She grabbed the radio and attempted to call to dispatch, but nothing sounded. "Great," she muttered. She fished her cell phone off the floorboard and the screen lit up. "No service." She looked out the front window and turned off her windshield wipers. There was nothing she could do for the moment. The only choice was to wait it out until the rain stopped and then she'd walk until she could gather a signal. Tired, defeated, and beyond frustrated, she leaned her head back and closed her eyes.

A horn honking woke her at half past six in the morning. She blinked, the fog from her breath clouding her windows and hindering her view of who'd happened to see her truck. Stifling embarrassment, she opened the truck door and slid out, her boots landing in over a foot of sludge.

"Well, good morning, Warden Keller." Clint Hastings stood next to his truck, the door ajar as he surveyed her predicament with a smug smile. "Long night?"

"You could say that." Bailey, relieved someone had found her, surveyed his nicely pressed shirt and crisp jeans. He wasn't dressed for work. He looked polished and put together and quite appealing. She shimmied away that thought. "What are you doing here?"

"I was headed to Sheffield for parts. Took the scenic route. You alright? No bumps or bruises?"

"I'm fine." She sighed, her tiredness no doubt showing through. "Just stuck."

"Let me get the straps, we'll pull ya out." He walked up to her, his eyes washing over every inch of her. Though a small thrill ran up her spine, she knew it was his way of checking for injury. Appeased by his appraisal, he nodded and walked back to his truck and opened his toolbox. He pulled out straps and began linking her truck to his. "Come on." He opened his passenger door and she hopped inside. It smelled masculine; a touch of hardworking male mixed with the underlying hint of cologne that matched the man behind the wheel. He shifted into gear, the hard pull on the back of his truck spinning his wheels on the slick road. He paused a moment, rotated the steering wheel and tried again. The truck lunged forward as one of the straps broke. He muttered under his breath something indecipherable, and she withheld her own groan of disappointment. "Hold on." He unbuckled his seat belt and walked to the rear of the truck to survey the broken strap.

She rolled down the window. "What can I do?"

"Get behind the wheel. I'll rig this up again and when I say go, pull forward."

She hopped into his driver seat, scooting as close to the steering wheel as possible without having to move his seat position. Her feet barely reached the pedals as she waited for his signal.

"Go," he called, and she shifted into drive. She felt his truck slowly move forward and could see her truck slowly trying to tug its way out of the deep, muddy trench. Glancing back towards the front, she gasped as she realized how close she was to driving off the opposite embankment and turned the wheel to avoid the mud on the other side. The quick change in direction had her overcompensating and she drove his truck right into the ditch in front of her own. "Oh, dear Lord." Her hands shook as she nervously awaited the wrath of Clint.

He ran up to the window. "What happened?"

"I—"

She could see the frustration on his face, but instead of lashing out at her, he waved for her to shift back into gear. "See if you can get it out." He untied the straps from his truck to hers and waited, but his tires spun. He ran back up to the window. "Alright, wait here. I'm going to gather some rocks. I've got a jack, I'll get the wheels up, lay the rocks, and give it some grip. If we can get my truck out, then we'll attempt to do the same with yours while I can pull it." He walked up and down the road, gathering rocks and boulders, big enough pieces to offer support for his task. She felt the truck lift as he pumped the jack, and she watched in the rearview mirror as he worked, feeling completely useless. She hopped out of the truck. "I can help."

He pointed. "Lay the rocks." He started laying them as well, and then he lowered the truck and jacked up the other side. After a half hour of gathering rocks, he motioned towards the truck. Breathless, Clint rested his hands on his hips. "Alright, give it a go. I'm going to push from behind to see if we can get it up on the road."

"Okay." She hustled back into his truck, scooted forward on the seat, and shifted into drive. She could hear him groan as he pushed with all his might, the tires gaining traction on the rocks. The truck bolted forward back onto the road and Bailey slammed on the brakes to keep it from careening off the opposite bank. She did not see Clint in the rearview mirror, and in a panic, jumped out of the truck and rounded the bed. His hands, wrist deep in mud, pushed his entire body out of the slosh. She couldn't help the laugh that bubbled forth at the sight of him covered from ankle to face in mud. He squinted in disapproval at her as she covered her mouth with her hand. "I'm sorry."

He picked up his dirty cowboy hat off the ground and tossed it into the bed of his truck, his town clothes completely destroyed. He opened his toolbox again and removed a different set of straps. "Let's try this again, shall we?" He set about tying her truck to his and then began removing their rock collection to go under her wheels.

She watched him a moment, his usual swagger tampered down by the moisture, the mud, and exertion. She liked it. She hadn't pegged Clint as chivalrous, but just now she felt like giving him a big hug of thanks. She would hold back, of course, but she couldn't help feeling impressed by his willingness to help her, no matter how dirty, muddy, or frustrated he became.

By the time she crawled behind his truck wheel again, another hour had passed, and Clint was starting to drag. But he still pushed the rear of her truck as hard as he could, his long legs spread and anchored in the ditch for support. For twenty minutes, they attempted to move her truck, and when she'd almost given up hope, she heard a wrangled scream of effort from behind her truck and a slight give and movement. She gunned his truck forward and her truck climbed from the muddy ruts and out onto the road. She cheered, jumping out of the truck. Clint sat in the mud, his arms resting on his knees as he panted and recovered from his unexpected workout.

"We did it!" Bailey nudged his shoulder, and a slight smile covered his face as he slowly pushed himself to his feet.

"Yeah. We did. Now help me out of this ditch because my muscles are like jelly." He placed a hand on her shoulder for support and they slipped and climbed their way up to the road.

"I don't know how to thank you or repay you." Bailey watched as his tired hands worked to untie the straps from his truck and hers. He folded them neatly and tucked them back into his toolbox.

He glanced at his watch and then swiped a thumb over the face of it to clear the mud. "By the time we get back to the main road and drive to Parks it will be lunchtime. You owe me lunch at Sloppy's."

"Oh." Bailey's brows lifted. "I wasn't headed to Parks today."

"You are now, Warden."

She reached forward, brushing her fingertips over his chin. His blue eyes sharpened, and she realized what she'd done. Blushing, she held up her fingers. "You had mud." She took a cautious step away from him, her own pulse kicking up ten notches at the contact. "Sloppy's it is."

H

Chapter Nine

Clint pulled into a front parking spot outside of Sloppy's Diner and waved a greeting to Roughneck Randy on the porch as he climbed out of his truck.

"My goodness." Randy looked him up and down. "You wrassle some cows, Clint?"

Clint smirked and shook his hand as Warden Keller pulled in next to his truck and hopped out looking as water worn as he did. Randy's brows lifted at the sight of her and then he let loose a wheezy laugh. "I see. Wasn't no cow you were wrasslin', huh?" He tipped the bill of his cap towards Bailey. "Warden."

Bailey politely smiled. "Hello."

"Got yerself a troublemaker here, ya know." Randy nodded towards Clint and grinned, showcasing his toothless smile.

"So I've heard." Bailey rested her hands on her hips. "But today he's been a law-abiding citizen."

"Oooooweeee," Randy, shifting in his worn-out chair, slapped whatever was in arm's length and happened upon Clint's pant leg. "Your reputation done got the warden after ya."

Clint chuckled at the pleased and amused response from Randy and then looked to Bailey. "All part of my plan." Clint winked and flashed an arrogant smirk her direction, leaving Randy in hoots of laughter as they walked inside.

Ruby glanced up from behind the bar and froze in her wiping of the counter tops. It was still an hour before her usual lunch rush, so that gave her more than enough time to soak in his disastrous appearance and give him a hard time. He saw her eyes dance and knew it was coming. "What on Earth happened to you?" She leaned over the bar to look at his hands. "Not in handcuffs, so that's a good sign. What did you do?" She looked to Bailey for explanation and Bailey, tired, plopped into one of the open seats at the bar.

"I'll have you know, Ruby 'Sloppy' Cole, that I rescued a damsel in distress." Clint nodded towards Bailey as he sat down beside her.

Ruby crossed her arms unconvinced. "Oh, really?"

"Yep. Just ask said damsel." Clint turned, his eyes dancing over Bailey's embarrassed features as she nodded.

"It's true, though I hate to admit it."

"What happened?" Ruby asked.

"This rain just took me by surprise last night. I slid off the road and into the ditch out in the middle of nowhere, and cowboy here found me this morning."

"Wait—" Clint looked at her in surprise. "You've been there since last night?"

"Yes," she answered wearily.

"Why didn't you tell me that?" he asked.

"Didn't really come up in the midst of mud, rocks, and rain."

"Well, it should have." Clint handed her a menu. "You're probably hungrier than I am. Ruby, it's on me, whatever she wants."

Ruby whipped out her notepad with a grin. "Got it. What will it be, Warden?"

"Her name is Bailey," Clint corrected.

"And I'm Ruby, and you mostly call me Sloppy."

Clint rolled his eyes as he rested his cowboy hat on the seat beside him.

"I am pretty hungry," Bailey admitted. "Maybe that awesome burger I had last time. Where is it?" she scanned the menu. "Ah, that one." She pointed and Ruby wrote it down.

"And you, Clint? Your usual?"

He rubbed his chin, flaky, dried mud crumbling to his lap. He stopped as soon as he saw it and then looked at his hands. His knuckles and nails were caked with grime. "Yeah, the usual. I need to go wash up."

"Use the back room." Ruby pointed over her shoulder to the side room off the kitchen that was only meant for employees. "Better scrubbing gear in there." She eyed Bailey. "You too, Warden."

Bailey looked at her hands, and her cheeks flushed at the call-out. "I'll have your drinks waitin' on ya when you get back."

Clint stood and Bailey followed him to the door not far from the bar. A large, stainless steel sink with a mirror above it and a side table were the only items in the small hallway, along with hooks along the wall for jackets, aprons, and purses. Clint turned on the water, testing its temperature before pouring a large dollop of soap in his hands. He set about scrubbing between his fingers. Bailey reached for the soap, and he lifted it to hand it to her, her hand softly brushing his. He caught a brief glimpse of his reflection and froze. Looking head-on into the mirror, he cringed. "Wowza."

Bailey followed his gaze and her eyes shot wide at her own appearance before a nervous laugh bubbled out of her. "Oh my."

"When you said I was covered, I didn't realize I was this covered." Clint laughed and shook his head as he went back to scrubbing his hands. "And you took me out in public like this?"

"It was your idea." Bailey giggled as he nudged her with his hip. "I look rough too. People are going to think we swam here. "I can't believe my hair." She pulled a small dirt clod from her blonde hair and let it wash away in the sink.

"I think you look cute." Clint gripped his hands together quickly under the water, shooting a small stream up at her. She jumped to dodge it, bumping into him.

"Hey now."

"Come on, Warden. What's a little more water gonna do?" Clint leaned his face down towards the sink and splashed water over his face, rubbing away what he could. When he raised up, Bailey stared intently at his face. "What?"

That pretty, pink tinge washed over her cheeks again. Though curious, Clint wouldn't scrutinize himself further until she confessed what she was thinking. He grabbed a few paper towels to dry his face, studying her between dabs.

"Nothing." She accepted the few towels he'd torn off for her. "I just kind of liked seeing you covered in mud."

"Is that so?" He took a step closer to her and leaned forward a bit, his presence looming over her.

She shoved him on her way to the door and laughed. "Not like that." She turned at the door and grinned. "Anyone ever tell you you're arrogant?"

"All the time." Unperturbed, he followed her out as she slid into her seat and eagerly took a sip of the sweet tea Ruby had promised.

"And it doesn't bother you?"

"No. Why should it?" Clint shrugged his shoulders. "I am sometimes. I know it. And when I'm not, I know that too. What people think of me is their business, not mine."

"Hmm." Her eyes followed him as he took a drink of his own tea.

"What? Did I miss some mud?" He swiped a few fingers over his cheek, and she grabbed his hand to bring it down from his face.

"No," she chuckled. "Well, yes, there's still mud, but that's not why I'm looking at you."

"Distracted by my beauty, Warden?"

She shoved his shoulder, "Stop it."

Ruby walked up at their playful banter and her eyes bounced between them. Clint's face sobered as if being caught by a scolding mother.

"So…" Ruby leaned back against the back counter across from them. "Lawrence said you never showed up for work today."

"I was a little busy." Clint pointed at Bailey.

"I can see that. But did you not think to let one of them know?"

"I didn't have cell service. We were on Refflin Road. And I was too busy bein' a knight in shining armor to think about my phone." He reached into his shirt pocket and patted his chest, realizing his phone wasn't there. He looked heavenward, praying it wasn't lost in the ditch somewhere. "You tell them I'm alive and well, will ya?"

She fished her phone from her back pocket and sent a lengthy text to the family group text.

"Ruby's my future sister-in-law," Clint explained.

"I heard." Bailey nodded towards the ring on Ruby's hand. "Congratulations."

"Don't congratulate her too much. She's marryin' Lawrence."

Ruby laughed and beamed proudly despite the insult to her intended. "You're just jealous you didn't snatch me up when you had the chance."

Clint shook his head. "No way. You were never on my radar."

"Oh, right." Ruby patted a hand over her hair, "I forget, I'm not blonde."

"Besides, Lawrence always had a soft spot for you. It was like a silent agreement that none of us ever pursue you. You were his from when we were kids."

His comment hit home, and Ruby's eyes held warmth, love, and stars at the thought of his brother.

"That's really sweet." Bailey smiled at his friend.

"Oh, it is," Ruby sighed happily. "Even if it means I have to put up with the likes of Clint from here on out."

"You did anyway."

"True. Might as well make it official." Ruby winked at him, and she turned her attention to Bailey. "Need anything else?"

Bailey shook her head.

"Good deal. I'm going to make the rounds." Ruby hurried off and Clint watched as she greeted the next customers who walked into the diner.

~

"I like her." Bailey took another sip of her tea. "And I love this tea."

"Yeah, Slop's pretty alright."

"Just out of curiosity though," She spun her stool to angle towards him as they talked. "why do you call her Sloppy? Seems a bit rude."

"Rude?" Clint looked completely flabbergasted at the suggestion. "It's sweet."

Bailey guffawed. "How is being called Sloppy sweet?"

"It's a pet name."

"That the entire community uses?"

"Exactly. See Ruby was a little bitty thing growin' up. Still is, I guess, if you think about it. But she was this rough and tumble little girl, cute and spunky, who was always wearin' holes in the knees of her pants, or rippin' her pretty white hose for church, or divin' headfirst into mud puddles. She was always sloppy. So that's what she became. It's not meant to be mean. We just all loved that about her."

"I see." Bailey looked up as the woman of conversation slid two plates in front of them.

"Eat up, kids."

Bailey breathed in the tantalizing aroma of her burger appreciatively and her stomach growled. Clint leaned back in amusement and stared at her. "Wow. Don't eat my arm off."

She laughed as she picked up the burger and noticed some dirt and grime still on her arms and hands. "I'm still filthy."

"Well, when you wallow with pigs, expect to get dirty." Ruby tilted her head towards Clint as he tossed his napkin at her. She laughed as she hurried off.

"Despite the mess and craziness of last night and this morning, I am grateful we're getting rain. It's been too hot lately." Bailey popped a French fry into her mouth and savored.

"Agreed. Summer's going to be a torcher." He swiveled her direction, his eyes lighting up. "Say, what does a warden do in the summer? I don't think I really know."

Surprised that he'd ask her such a question, she swiped a napkin over her lips. "Oh, well, lots of things really."

"Write a bunch of tickets?" He smirked.

"Not quite, though there is plenty of that. Last summer, I was down in Eagle Pass helping border patrol with drug cartel crossings in the Rio Grande. I spent most of my time in a boat making arrests or being shot at. This summer will be a nice reprieve, as I'm assigned to stay in this area."

"Wait, shot at? What?"

She nodded. "It happens. The cartel doesn't play around when they're trying to smuggle drugs, weapons, or even humans across the border into the U.S. Sometimes the border patrol or local law enforcement need more hands on deck. We also assist local sheriff's departments if they need us."

"I had no idea."

"We *are* law enforcement," she reminded him.

"Well, yeah, but I didn't realize you guys actually did that stuff too. I thought you were just land and wildlife oriented. What'd your folks think about you workin' in such a dangerous position last year?"

"My dad." She corrected. "Well, he wasn't too crazy about it." She smiled. "But he knows I love what I do, and he supports me, even if he has to say a few extra prayers every now and then."

"Wow." Clint reached over and squeezed her hand, his thumb lightly brushing over the top of her knuckles. "Yeah…" He stared at her a moment longer before releasing his hold and turning back to his meal. Bailey's heart hammered in her chest as she tried to nonchalantly focus her attention back to her own plate. They ate in silence for a few minutes. "You hunt?"

The turn in conversation caught her off guard. "Not as much as I'd like, but yes. I grew up hunting with my dad."

Clint finished his meal and nudged his plate away from him before turning his bright blue eyes back on her. She was starting to love looking into those eyes, and that scared her. "Come dove hunting with me."

"It's August."

"I know."

"Dove season isn't until September." She narrowed her eyes at him.

He laughed. "I know that too. I meant in September. Opening weekend. How 'bout it?"

The idea intrigued her. She hadn't been hunting in a while, and she didn't mind the thought of hanging out with Clint outside of work. Maybe then she'd be able to relax more in his presence. But did she really want to cross that line with him? Did she want to become friends? Or keep their relationship professional?

"Warden?"

"Sure. Opening weekend, it is."

"Great. It's a date." His handsome smile lit up his face and he waved towards Ruby for the check.

"This is on me, remember?" Bailey accepted the ticket from Ruby and fished in her pocket for cash. "I owe you for helping me out of the ditch."

"And what do you owe me for gettin' my truck stuck too?" Clint asked, a sly smirk sliding onto his face.

"A hearty apology," Bailey replied, making Ruby giggle from the register at her dry response.

"Well, that's just lame." Clint straightened in his chair. "I was hopin' for a kiss or somethin'." He tapped his cheek and Bailey shook her head on a nervous laugh.

"I'm sorry to disappoint you. Besides, I'd hate to harm your reputation. I am a warden. Not sure if you'd like people seeing you cozied up with the likes of me."

"My daddy used to always say to keep skunks and bankers at a distance. He never said anything about pretty game wardens. I'm willing to risk it." Clint's eyes sparkled as he teased her, and she stood, ignoring his advance.

"Good advice." She smoothed a hand down the front of her dirty uniform. "Thank you, Clint, for helping me today." She extended her hand towards him. "I'd still be out there if you hadn't found me."

"Oh, I'm sure someone would have started lookin' for ya sooner or later. But it is best practice to have the best tracker in your corner." He gripped her hand, tugging her towards him a bit. "Don't forget about September." He held her gaze, his face growing serious.

She felt the rush of warmth travel up her arm and tingle the nerves near her heart. And though she wanted to stare a little longer into his blue eyes, she nodded, backed away, and hurried toward her truck.

H

Chapter Ten

"You and the warden? Now that's definitely not something I saw coming." Lawrence punched Clint's shoulder on a laugh. "Cal was pretty ticked you didn't get parts, but after Ruby texted us a picture of you and the warden at the diner, all was forgiven."

"I'm glad my choice in company could divert his wrath."

"It wasn't the warden, it was you." Lawrence pointed to Clint's messy appearance. "We could tell she wasn't lyin', or that you were lyin' to her."

"Clint," Seth walked up holding a notepad in his hand and tapping a pen against it. He smiled. "Helena's dad called today. Not only do we have him booked for November, but he recommended a couple of buddies that are interested too. Wanted to run them by you to see if we wanted to get their hunts booked."

Liking that Seth was spending the drizzly day working on their joint effort of a hunting operation, Clint nodded. "Let me shower and come by the house."

"Will do. I've got to go help Hayes at the stables for a bit and then I'll come over." Seth started to walk off and Lawrence grabbed him in a choke hold and rubbed a fist into his hair.

Seth grunted in frustration as he tried to wriggle free of Lawrence's strong grasp, Clint laughing as he watched. Seth pulled away and glowered at his brother. "Lawrence, I ain't ten anymore. Knock it off."

Clint and Lawrence smirked at his defiance, and Seth hurried towards his truck.

"He'll always be ten." Lawrence ran a hand through his shaggy hair. "So, how was Ruby today?"

Clint tilted his head at his brother's question. "Good. Why? You haven't talked to her?"

"I think I upset her," Lawrence admitted. "She wanted to go out tomorrow, and I sort of shut her down. I just don't feel like it this weekend. Anyway, she was a bit huffy, so I didn't know if I'd clouded her day."

"I think all is forgiven. At the mention of your name at lunch she was still rather whimsy and in love with you, so good job not screwing it up too much."

Relief washed over Lawrence's face. "Good to know. Thanks." He rubbed a palm over his chest. "I don't know what I'd do now if she ever decided to pitch me to the curb."

"I don't think you'll ever have to find out," Clint assured him.

"So, what's this thing with the cute warden?" Lawrence asked. "You diggin' her?"

"I might be." Clint's eyes gleamed.

"I'm surprised," Lawrence admitted. "Figured you and Kara would try to work things out."

"She's dating Jimmy and they're happy. Besides, Kara was just fun to flirt with. I never saw anything serious happening there."

"But you do with the warden?"

"Don't know. But I'm going to find out. I'm going to take her dove hunting here in a couple weeks."

"Oh really?" Lawrence's brows lifted and disappeared under his hat. "A little one on one, huh? Dangerous territory, brother. Dangerous territory."

"Why's that?"

Lawrence cleared his throat and held up a finger. "First, Graham takes Julia to walk by the creek, she kisses him. Second, Calvin working on Alice's house, and she walks in, just the two of them, bam! More kissing. Third, Philip takes Helena for a walk in the rain... I know, he's always been the dramatic gesture one, but boom! Kissing. I take Ruby to the creek to fish, we get a little cozy at the bridge, and shazam! Kissing. So this little "dove hunting" idea of yours, might just turn into somethin' a little different if you're not careful."

Clint laughed as Lawrence, pleased with his synopsis, grinned.

"Or better yet, I'll go with ya. I've never hunted with a warden before."

"No. You're not going," Clint ordered.

"Ahh... so you *want* a little alone time with her. I see, I see." Lawrence held up his hands in surrender. "I get it. I won't hinder your mojo then."

Lawrence took a step towards his truck and then paused, turning back around, his tone serious. "So Ruby wasn't upset?"

"Nope," Clint reassured him, and Lawrence gave a quick nod of his head in thanks before walking towards his truck. Clint watched him drive off, chuckling to himself. Little Ruby Cole had his brother wrapped around her pretty little finger. All the new women in his life seemed to have his brothers bewitched.

It all started with Julia, but no one could blame Graham for pursuing Jewels. She swept onto the ranch with pretty dresses, a pretty face, and pretty personality to boot. They were all better because of her presence. And Graham, despite him being hard most of his life, deserved happiness. He deserved someone to care about him and see about him. Clint was still shocked a woman actually wanted to, but he was grateful and happy Julia signed on to do it. She was head over heels for Graham, and that feeling was mutual.

Cal and Alice surprised him too. There'd always been a little something brewing there, but for polar opposites to connect so well was equally mind-blowing. But Cal, ever the patient one, could handle Alice's moodiness and abruptness. He could handle her screamin' and bossin' like nobody else could. And not only handle it but love it. Clint waved as Cal drove by heading towards Graham's house.

Then pretty, put-together Helena breezed into the feed store and rocked Philip's world. It wasn't surprising Phil would find a sweetheart. His brother was the only one who dated much since he was closest to actual people, but it happened so quickly. All of them had, really.

Lawrence and Ruby taking their friendship to the next level and already engaged left his head spinning. He kept waiting for them to spring a wedding date on them all, but so far it hadn't happened.

And then Hayes falling for Ally and little Ava. Hayes was well on his way to family town already and he seemed so at peace with it, as though a few months ago and his life before them was but a distant memory. Hayes loved his girls, and like the rest of his brothers, their love made him a better man. Wasn't hard to do with Hayes, Clint admitted, since he was always the kindest of the bunch. But he could see small hints of a woman's touch on his brother's life. On all their lives.

Clint leaned against the fence, eyes surveying the view of the ranch and soaked the place in. Could he be next? Was his attraction to Bailey different than the other women he'd dated in the past? He wasn't sure, but she seemed to be. For one, she wasn't shallow, and if he were honest, he'd admit that his flings and flirtations in the past were a bit superficial. But he had also never invited any of them out to the ranch, and Bailey had been here multiple times. Not on his invite, but she'd held her own amongst his family. She held her own with *him*. He rubbed a hand over his tired face. He needed to shower. He needed to get his clothes to soaking so that maybe he could salvage his good shirt. But the thought of washing away the morning's events disappointed him. It'd been a pain, pushing the back of the truck in the mud, but the time with Bailey had been nice. Fun, even. And he wasn't quite ready to see that wash down the drain.

~

Bailey turned into the entrance of the 7H Ranch and took a deep breath. She hadn't seen Clint since her whole truck in the ditch situation a few weeks ago. Sure, they'd exchanged a few texts, but nothing more than a simple, 'Hey, how's it going?'. And her work had kept her busy all along the Pecos that she hadn't ventured into Parks until now. She wasn't quite sure where to meet him, so she pulled into the front of the main house, which she knew belonged to Graham and Julia. Julia stepped out onto the porch with a friendly wave. Bailey hopped out of her truck. "I'm here to meet Clint, but he didn't tell me where to go."

"No worries. Come on in." Julia held the screen door open, and Bailey walked in to find Graham standing at the stove sauteing vegetables that were no doubt being prepped for their supper.

"Warden." His brow lifted at her unexpected visit.

"She's here to see Clint." Julia's voice hitched at the last of her sentence as her eyes danced towards her husband. A small smirk lifted Graham's lips at her hopefulness of another brother finding a girl.

"I reckon he'll be up here in a few, then." Graham turned his attention back to the stove.

"I'm sorry to intrude on you guys during supper."

"Not supper yet." Julia waved away her concern. "Can I get you a tea or anything?"

"No, thank you. That's okay."

The screen door whooshed open and Alice, covered in hay, walked in with a pungent stench lingering around her.

"Whoa." Julia covered her nose and mouth as Graham looked his friend up and down.

"What happened?" he asked.

"Don't ask." Alice rolled her eyes and walked to the refrigerator and withdrew a cold beer. "It's been a long day."

"I'd say." Julia motioned to her stained and dirty appearance. "I'm sorry I wasn't there today."

"Don't be. Jimmy held down the office. I was over in Sanderson preg checking cows today."

Julia's nose scrunched in disgust.

"Yeah," Alice agreed, holding up her arm that had been gloved most of the day. "All. Day. Long."

"Good results?" Graham asked, and Alice rolled her eyes.

"Yes. Though it's probably one of my least favorite things to do." Her eyes flashed over to Bailey, and she did a double take. "Warden Keller?"

Bailey gave a small wave.

"Almost didn't recognize you out of your uniform. What brings you here?"

"Clint," Julia repeated, her tone still holding a touch of excitement.

"What'd he do this time? I swear, Graham, you're going to have to talk to him if he keeps getting into trouble. I kind of thought he'd straightened up, trying to prove all this hunting business success to you." Alice ranted and then sighed as if there was nothing any of them could do.

"Apparently he hasn't done anything wrong," Julia offered, then sat at the table, resting her chin in her hand.

The sound of a truck pulling up to the house had Bailey turning to peer out the screen door. Hayes walked up the steps, removing his hat as his boots hit the porch. He knocked on the doorframe.

"Come on in, Hayes," Julia called.

He stepped inside, his eyes adjusting to the interior and to all the extra faces in the room. "Bad time?"

Julia shook her head. "Never."

"What's up?" Graham asked.

"I'm heading to Sheffield tomorrow to spend the day with Ally and Ava. Plan on leaving early in the mornin'."

"Need someone to feed the horses?" Graham asked.

"Yes."

Julia perked up and nodded. "We'll do it."

Graham turned his gaze on his wife, and she grinned. He nodded to Hayes that he and Julia would see to it.

"Thanks." His eyes washed over Bailey. "I'm sorry." He shifted his hat to his left hand and extended his right. "Not sure if we've met. I'm Hayes Hastings."

Bailey shook his hand. "Bailey Keller."

"You've seen her," Alice interrupted. "The game warden."

Recognition sparked in Hayes's eyes. "Oh, right. Sorry. I didn't recognize you."

Bailey, starting to feel somewhat out of place, felt a sigh of relief when she saw Clint's truck pull up next to hers outside. Her pulse leapt when his eyes locked with hers through the screen door. His face split into a wide smile when he entered.

"Evenin'." He removed his hat, bending down to kiss Julia's cheek. He gave a wave towards a filthy Alice.

"Clint, when the warden starts makin' house calls, it's time for an intervention," Alice teased.

Clint grinned and reached for Bailey's hand and tugged her towards him. "I'm stealin' her away for some dove hunting this evening."

Graham turned from the stove, and crossed his arms over his chest and leaned against the countertop. "What pasture?"

"Over by the nopalito tank."

"Good spot." Graham offered an affirmative shake of his head. "Good luck."

Clint nudged her out the door and down the steps, his pace quick and eager. "Best to leave before they start askin' questions, or worse, invite themselves along."

"I need to grab my gun." Bailey reached into her truck, removed a camo case and slid it into his backseat before hopping in the front.

Clint watched her, his eyes roaming over her boots, jeans, and lightweight button up shirt. "Ready?" he asked.

"Yep."

He drove them to one of the most eastern pastures of the ranch, Bailey enjoying the view of distant hills and cows spotted throughout. She noticed various houses tucked here and there, all landscaped and pristine. Clint pointed to one over the hill. "That's my place." A farm-style home with cedar beams across the porch and a sleeping dog on the porch.

"Looks picturesque."

"I like it." He turned and headed towards the neighboring pasture and parked. He hopped out, pulling his tailgate down and lining up his ammunition. He reached for his well-used Remington 870, 12-gauge shotgun and set it on the bed. Bailey retrieved her gun case and laid it up on the tailgate and unclipped the locks. When she opened the case, Clint whistled under his breath.

"What in the world?" He held a hand to his chest. "Is this... it is." He reverently ran his finger over the action. "A Ruger red label, over and under..." He bent down to peer at it closer. "Walnut stock, engraved action." He touched the engraving of her name and a date underneath.

"It was a gift." She proudly pulled it out of the case and handed it to him. He turned it over in his hands to admire the wood grain and inscription. "My dad gave it to me the day I graduated from the Academy. It was his gun, taught me to shoot with that one too."

Clint shook his head in bewilderment. "You know what I learned to shoot with? An old breakover single-barrel Mossberg."

"A decent gun for teaching," Bailey acknowledged.

"But not a red label!" Clint laughed and handed her gun back to her. "You've got yourself a beauty there, Warden. Almost too pretty to use. Don't want it to get muddy."

"What good's a gun if you're not going to use it?"

"But that gun is worth around $2000!"

"And I'll clean it if it gets dirty. I take it apart, clean it, put it back together, put it away each time so that it stays this pretty." She looked up and caught him staring at her with a slack jaw. "What?"

"I think I could stand here and listen to you talk about that gun all day." He weakened his knees a moment and pretended to faint and she laughed, giving him a shove.

"I thought you brought me out here to hunt some birds?"

"Oh, right." Clint grabbed his shotgun. "Guess we better get to it then." He pointed to one tree, and she flipped open a dove stool and sat while he did the same at another. They'd sit, though not for much longer if her watch was correct, and they'd patiently wait for the birds to come to the water before making their way to roost. And then, it was game on.

H

Chapter Eleven

He tucked his gun, aimed, shot, and watched the dove fall to the ground. Before he collected it, he aimed and hit another. He heard Bailey's gun shoot as well, but didn't take his eyes off of his own birds so as not to lose sight of where the birds fell. He walked out and retrieved them. "Two for me, Warden." He could see her frustration at missing her own targets and he grinned. He nestled back against the tree and waited a moment before he saw several birds coming on the wind. "You're two-o-clock, Warden."

He watched as she raised her gun and took the shot, missing yet again, but firing again, determined to hit the bird on the second round. She clipped it and he shot it to finish the job.

"I had it."

"Now, I'd hate to see you waste three bullets on one bird." Clint's teeth flashed in a devilish smile before he settled his back against the tree and waited. He watched as she did the same, though he noticed she closed her eyes when the breeze picked up. He watched as she visibly relaxed and then stared at the setting sun. They only had an hour or so of daylight left and he hoped they had better luck and more birds arrived or their trip wouldn't be much of one. His hope was to feast on dove afterwards. He pulled his cellphone out of his pocket and shot Lawrence a text about lighting his grill for him so that it was hot by the time they were finished. If they had enough birds, they'd eat dove. If they didn't, he had some burgers in the freezer he could toss on.

Lawrence: *"Just come to my place. Cal, Al, Ruby, and Seth are over here. We're grilling steaks. I'll keep the grill warm."*

Not quite what he had in mind, but a nice Friday night hangout on Lawrence's back patio sounded pretty good too. Bailey's gun sounded and brought his attention back to hunting. He watched as a bird fell to the ground and she fetched it.

"While you were sleeping, I got us a bird."

Clint bit back a grin, liking the taunting side of the warden. "That one wasn't even worth killin'. Barely any meat on him."

She held up the large dove. "Give me a break, Hastings, it's bigger than all of yours combined."

He guffawed and liked the bright smile she flashed his way.

As the sun continued to set and the sky lit in its glorious shades of purples, oranges, pinks, and reds, the birds flew in a steady stream and Clint and Bailey both fired at will. When he'd reached his limit, Clint stopped and gathered up his bundle.

"You clocking out?" Bailey asked. "Already?"

"I hit my limit. And you hit an extra two." He pointed to her small pile.

"No, I didn't. I haven't even hit my limit y— wait." She fisted a hand on her hip as he chuckled and tossed two birds on her pile.

"Just consider it as you're one step closer to your fifteen."

"Clint—" She shook her head.

"Come on, there has to be some incentive to hunting with the warden." Curious to see if she'd let his lapse slide, he knelt in the grass and worked on lining up her birds to get a full count.

"Fine. They can count towards mine," Bailey acquiesced, and he shielded his eyes against the setting sun to look up at her. The fact she'd let it slide meant she'd enjoyed herself. "But I'm done, I think."

"We can be done. I have Lawrence keepin' the grill hot if we want to clean these up and have a meal." He stood, resting his empty gun against the tree as he gathered all the birds and placed them in a bucket to carry them towards the water tank. "We'll have to clean them first." He walked over to the nearest cattle water trough and Bailey followed. She withdrew a pair of game shears from her ammo bag, Clint impressed that she came prepared.

"I only have to clean six, right?" She grinned as she reached for the first bird.

"If you only want to eat six," he quipped.

She nudged him with her hip before clipping the first wing. She was quick, efficient, and skilled at handling the birds. And though they were both covered in feathers by the end of it, they'd successfully cleaned enough for them to have a nice supper.

Clint bagged up the meat and they rinsed their hands in the trough. "Ready?"

"I'm starving," Bailey admitted, and he was glad she seemed okay with continuing their evening together. When they reached his truck, he lowered the tailgate to put his stool and bucket inside.

"Whoa! Nice find!" Bailey's face lit up at the sight of the deer antlers he'd found with Hayes, Ally, and Ava.

"Thanks. I've been carting them around for a while meaning to run them up to Annie and Henry to show them."

"Promising signs."

"Oh yeah, great set of horns."

"You mean antlers," she corrected.

He chuckled as he shut the tailgate. "Come on now, you're in west Texas. We don't call them antlers and you know it. They're horns or sheds. Antlers…" He shook his head in dismay. "That's what city folk call them."

"Technically—"

"Don't bust out technicalities." Clint held up his hand and then placed their bag of meat into a cooler. "Want a beer?"

"Of course. Can't go dove hunting without a beer." She stood with her hands on her hips, her hair in a short ponytail, and feathers tucked within any crevice they could find: her collar, her blonde hair, her pockets. Her steady gaze stared at the horizon as the sun barely peeked over, and Clint couldn't remember ever seeing a woman so beautiful. He leaned forward and kissed her cheek and she bounced to attention, her hand flying to her face in surprise.

"W-what was that for?" Nervously, she flicked a feather from her shirt, and he grinned, handing her a beer.

She popped the tab and took a long sip.

"I think I love you already," he teased, pulling out his own can and doing the same. "Come on, we'll go whip us up some birds." He reached for her gun, and she handed it to him, allowing him to admire it once more before placing it in her case. "Still one of the prettiest things I've ever seen."

"Thanks." Bailey reached for her case, his hold not relinquishing when her hand gripped his over the handle.

"I meant you," Clint replied, his eyes soaking in her face mere inches from his. He hesitated a moment, wanting to warm her up to the idea of a kiss, but his window of opportunity was slipping away. He could feel it in the slight tug of her case in his hand. He let go. Perhaps he was reading too much into their time together.

She started to walk towards the passenger door and paused, turning to face him. "You frustrate me."

Not expecting the annoyance in her tone, Clint straightened, resting his elbow on the bed of his truck to find out what he'd done to upset her.

"Well?" she asked. "Do you have anything to say about that?"

"Not really. I frustrate a lot of people."

"And you're okay with it?"

"I am who I am. What can I say?" He scratched his chin. "Though I'm a little confused as to how I've frustrated you in the last five minutes. I'm sorry if I've offended you somehow."

Bailey growled and stormed towards him, her head tilting back so she could meet his gaze. "You haven't offended me." Though her face was still flushed and her tone clipped, her eyes danced down to his lips.

He gently brushed a knuckle down her soft cheek, leaning closer towards her. She didn't back away. Instead, she placed a hand on his chest as his fingers slid to behind her neck. "Good." His voice rumbled as he tenderly pressed his lips to hers and she melted into him. He drove the kiss deeper, liking the fire he tasted beneath the surface, the annoyance and tension of the last few months unraveling in a soft wave of warmth and heat that wasn't from the west Texas weather. He pulled a breath away from her, his hands cupping her cheeks, and lightly pressed one more soft kiss to her lips before whispering, "So, can I shoot your gun?" He grunted on a laugh as her elbow found his ribs and she darted to hop into his truck.

~

Bailey hadn't felt giddy in ages. In fact, she couldn't even remember the last time she'd kissed a man and felt the pure pleasure of it down to the tips of her toes. Even the hairs on her head tingled from Clint's gentle touch. She hadn't meant to kiss him. She hadn't even meant to enjoy herself in his company. But there was something more to him than his reputation, or even his own opinion of himself. Deep down, he was a good man. His family was important to him. He loved the land. He loved to hunt. All great qualities. He didn't have to help her when her truck was stuck in the ditch, he just did. She bounced in the seat as they hit a large divot in the dirt road.

"Sorry about that. Cal hasn't made it out here in a while to maintain the roads." He glanced her direction, and a nervous smile lifted the corner of his lips. He reached across the console, hesitated a moment, and then slid his hand over hers. She looked down at her small hand, her fingers laced through his and felt a sense of ease she hadn't felt in some time.

"Clint—"

He cleared his throat and shook his hand free and placed it back on the steering wheel. "Sorry about that. I just... well, I— Nevermind. I get it."

"No, no..." She turned in her seat to face him. "It's nothing like that." She wound her hands in her lap and watched as he focused more intently on the dirt path in front of them and his jaw tensed. He was bracing himself for her rejection, and that thought softened something inside of her. She had no intention of ignoring what happened between them. "I was just going to say that I... I had a lot of fun this evening... with you."

He peeked from the corner of his eye and then glanced back at the road.

"So... thanks."

He pulled the truck to a stop in front of Lawrence's house, his brother's dog and Ruby's rushing towards them and barking. She could see the light tint of smoke drifting up from the grill behind the house and knew his family was waiting for them, but she wanted to clear the air. She also wasn't quite ready to end their time together, though that thought somewhat terrified her.

He turned off the engine and placed his key on the dashboard. "I'll get the birds." He started to open his door and she grabbed his arm.

"Wait." When his blue eyes, disappointed and uncertain found hers, she gently rested her hand on his cheek, her thumb lightly brushing the corner of his mouth. The air thickened and she felt butterflies dance in her stomach. "I think I'm going crazy," she whispered. "Because all I want to do is kiss you again."

Clint sighed, moving his face out of her reach. He removed his cowboy hat and set it on the dash and ran a hand through his hair. "Well, Warden, you'd better do it now. Otherwise, we're going to have an audience." He pointed to Lawrence waving from the side of his house for them to come on back. Clint gave a wave of acknowledgement and his brother disappeared around the house. When he turned back around, she planted a firm kiss on his lips. His mouth parted into a smile as her stomach let out a loud grumble. He placed his thumb on her chin and rested his forehead against hers. "Come on, let's go eat." He jumped out of his truck, rushing around the front to open her door for her. When she stepped out, he kissed her again. "Mmm mmm *mmm*! I don't think I will ever get enough." He winked at her as he pulled their dove bag from his cooler and let her recover from the blush he'd caused.

"We should definitely talk about this," Bailey suggested.

"We should wait."

"Why?"

"Because right now, Bailey Keller, you just like me. By the end of the night, you're going to love me. Let's talk then." He closed his cooler with a thud and confidently tugged her toward him. "Now, let me bewitch you with my culinary talents." He led her around the back of Lawrence's house and more faces than she expected stared back at them. Alice's eyes flashed down to their joined hands and she bit back a smirk as Calvin stood politely to greet them.

"Glad you guys could make it."

Ruby walked out of the sliding glass door from inside and placed a tray with crackers, cheese, and smoked sausage on the table. "Perfect timing, guys. Law is seasoning the steaks. Clint, if you want to get the doves inside and whip them up, we'll throw those on first. Hi, Bailey."

"Hi. I can help prep." She looked up at Clint and he shook his head.

"Nope. Lawrence and I will get it. You sit out here, enjoy a fresh beer, and relax."

"Pull up a seat." Alice nudged an empty chair with her foot. Having showered and changed from her full day of checking cows, the vet looked completely at ease among her friends. Cal lightly tugged on Alice's ponytail when he walked by to claim his own seat, while Ruby eased into another and propped her feet in what must have been Lawrence's empty chair.

"When the boys want to cook, you let them." Ruby slid a cold beer towards Bailey. "How was dove hunting?"

"Oh," Bailey tucked a loose fray of hair behind her ear. "It was good. Though Clint had better luck than I did."

"He sure did." Cal smirked and took a sip of his drink as Seth walked through the door holding a soda and a candy bar. His eyebrows raised at the sight of Bailey, and he swallowed his bite.

"Warden Keller."

"Hi." She offered a wave, having a hard time remembering the youngest Hastings brother's name.

"Seth," Alice reminded her. "And what are you doing? We're about to eat steak and you're chompin' on a chocolate bar?"

"I was hungry." He relaxed on top of a cooler and turned to Bailey. "Thanks for helping Clint and me with the groundwork of our hunting operation."

"I didn't do much." Bailey smiled. "Just some papers."

"Yeah, but you got us moving a bit faster. Clint was so pumped after talking to you and Mike. We've got the cooler and skinning shed ready. The hunts are booked for the most part. We have a couple of spots still open, but Clint's reserving those for some of Helena's dad's friends." Excitement had his right knee bouncing. That or the caffeine, she wasn't sure. But she liked Seth's friendly demeanor and enjoyed hearing the details of what Clint had been working on over the last few months. There was no lull in conversation with him, and until his head lunged forward from being shoved by Lawrence, Seth chatted almost nonstop.

"Give it a rest, Seth." Lawrence reached to tap the edge of his hat and realized he didn't wear one, so he saluted instead. "Warden."

"You can call me Bailey."

"You might as well get used to it," Alice suggested. "They rarely call me Alice. It's either Al or Doc."

"And I'm usually still called Slop or Sloppy," Ruby added.

"Only I'm allowed to call her Bailey." Clint walked up and set the tray of dove by the grill for Lawrence too cook. He'd spiced them, added sliced jalapeno, wrapped them in bacon and waited for his brother to throw them on the fire.

"You never call me Bailey." She looked over at him and his eyes grew serious.

"Yeah, well, that's changed now, hasn't it?"

"I'm liking the sounds of this." Ruby shimmied her shoulders. "I'm guessing we'll be seeing more of you around here."

"I—"

"Yes." Clint answered for her. "All the time."

"You're confident." Alice popped a cracker into her mouth and then sputtered. "Law, what is this?" She spit it out into her napkin.

Lawrence chuckled. "Jalapeno crackers. Just trying to give you and Cal a little spice."

"I'll stick to saltines." Alice stood and walked to the house. "Oh, and Annie stopped by Graham's earlier. She was upset the warden was here and you didn't tell her."

"Is there an alert system now?" Clint asked.

"When it comes to Annie there is." Cal grinned. "She was excited that the pretty warden seemed to be keeping you in line."

"I think she gives me too much credit," Bailey mumbled and had Clint shooting her a sly smile as he placed their dove on the grill.

"You are welcome to come to Sunday supper," Seth invited. "That should suffice for Annie."

Ruby's feet hit the deck. "Oooooh, you're right, Seth." She looked to Bailey. "Every Sunday after church we meet over at Annie's house for lunch. You should come."

"I'm not sure I'll be in the area, actually. I'm to be in Del Rio on Monday."

Clint's head popped up, his eyes concerned at the news; no doubt thinking of her stories from their lunch at Sloppy's about her work along the border. "For how long?" he asked.

"A few days. Then I'll be back in this area. It is dove season, so I'll be making the rounds. Checking licenses." She narrowed her gaze at him, and he smiled.

"Bummer." Ruby waved it away. "Well, we do it every Sunday, so eventually Clint will have to bring you. Annie would love it."

"And Annie is the best cook," Seth complimented. "Though Julia is a close second."

Lawrence cleared his throat, offended not to be included in the list as he placed steaks on the grill.

"And you make a pretty decent steak," Seth added.

"Decent." Lawrence shook his head in disappointment. "Beat him up, Cal. Or better yet, let's throw a chicken breast on here for him."

"No way." Seth laughed. "I want steak."

"Then you better think they're better than just *decent*." Lawrence, with no intention of changing the menu, continued placing the meat on the racks.

Clint sat next to Bailey and tapped her knee with his finger. "You good?" he asked softly.

She smiled and nodded, squeezing his hand in thanks for checking up on her. He turned his hand over, his wide palm and fingers swallowing hers. He started to lift it to his lips and then stopped. "Have you washed your hands yet?"

Giggling, she shook her head. "Not unless you count the cattle trough."

He grimaced and opted out of kissing the back of her hand and instead pulled her to her feet and walked her into the house.

H

Chapter Twelve

Clint's day started with the promise of excitement, glee, and pride. But when he reached the elk wallow and checked his cameras, he hadn't captured one photo of them watering on the ranch. Not that they weren't coming across the fence from Chandler's property, because they were. He had the tracks to prove it. Fresh ones. But because he'd chosen to be cheap. Stinkin' cheap. He growled and tossed the dead batteries from the game camera into the floorboard of his truck and replaced them, reprogramming the camera's settings to try again.

Seth walked up with the other cameras. "Both dead. Where'd you get your batteries?"

"Doesn't matter," Clint barked. "We'll replace them with better ones and check them more often."

Seth held his hands up to ward off Clint's temper and pulled the dead batteries from the other two cameras while Clint took his frustration out on driving a new metal fence t-post into the ground. He'd switch angles, strap the camera to the post, and hope for the best.

"You sure Chandler has elk?" Seth asked.

"Yes."

"Mike didn't say what properties had them," Seth pointed out. "Just that they'd been spotted in this area. You ask Bailey yet?"

"Nope. Don't need to."

"Why?"

"Because I know they're here." Clint's jaw flexed in frustration, his expression changing so that he looked more like Graham than himself. "I know tracks. And those are elk tracks."

"I'd still ask her." Seth held out a replenished camera and Clint snatched it from his hand.

"She's busy."

"I bet she'd take a call from you." Seth grinned and wriggled his eyebrows, not even that comment bringing a smile to Clint's face.

"It doesn't matter what Bailey says, Graham wants proof."

"He'd respect the word of a warden."

"Doesn't matter. She's busy."

"Something happen between you two since last week at Lawrence's?" Seth asked, curious as to why his brother's attitude wasn't as smitten as before.

"No," Clint replied quickly, though his eyes avoided Seth's. "Well, I don't know."

"What do you mean?"

"Look, I don't want to talk about this."

"Why not? I can't judge." Seth waved a hand over himself. "I don't have a girlfriend. Not like I can give advice. Just thought you might need to talk something out."

Clint puffed an irritated breath. "Fine. Things were great last weekend. Bailey and I, I thought, had sort of started somethin'. Then she's been busy with work this week, which I get, but I haven't heard a word from her. Not a call. Not a text."

Seth's lips twitched at his brother's anxiety over a woman treating him exactly the way he used to treat women in the past.

"I mean, not that I want her blowin' up my phone or expect more than what we've already established. I just thought there was something starting there."

"And you want something to start with the warden?"

"Obviously," Clint huffed. "Why would I have even initiated anything with her if I didn't?"

"You've *initiated* things with other women in the past and it's never gone anywhere. Why's she different?"

Clint stared off a moment, his eyes following a few cows as they grazed near the trough. *Why was Bailey different?*

"She's seen the real me and still likes me," Clint explained. "She's outdoorsy, loves to hunt, and she's tough when she needs to be."

"Pretty too," Seth added.

"*Beautiful,*" Clint corrected. "And small."

"Small?" Seth laughed. "Didn't realize that was a quality you were after."

"It wasn't. I just like it. I like that she's this little petite firecracker that can hold her own against a man like me, yet still needs help from time to time. Like when I helped her pull her truck out of the ditch. She needed me then, yet she was right there with me in the mud doing what she could to help herself out. She's not afraid to get dirty."

Seth leaned against the grill guard of Clint's truck, resting his boot on the bumper and listened.

"And I like her smile." Clint's tone lifted as though he'd just realized a new trait he appreciated, and his own lips raised into a smirk at the thought. "It's one of those that is somewhat rare because she's always serious, but when she gives you a full smile, it's like… wow." Clint went back to fumbling the batteries in the camera and slid the back in place. "Anyways, I like her. I do. And maybe I was thinking about getting' a little serious with her. But I don't know if she feels the same way. Aren't women supposed to blow up your phone when they have feelings for you? Or are interested?"

Seth shrugged. "Beats me. Single, remember?" He pointed at himself on a laugh. "But I don't remember Julia bombarding Graham with messages, though I do know they talked on the phone a lot. Alice, well, she always texted Cal. She had to boss him around at least once a day. And Ruby's pretty relaxed. Lawrence messages her all the time, though."

Clint grunted under his breath and sighed. "It's whatever, I guess. I may have just been readin' into things too much. I'm cool with casual. Heck, I'm good at it. The warden just struck me as a woman who didn't *do* casual, you know? Guess I was wrong."

"Or," Seth countered. "Just being devil's advocate here, but maybe she *is* just busy, like you say.

Perfect explanation. She's takin' down bad guys, ticketing the non-licensed folk, and battling the brush on poacher tracks. You never know. Maybe you'll hear from her this weekend once she's done in Del Rio."

"Yeah. You're probably right. I mean, why wouldn't she call me back, right?" Clint outstretched his arms and grinned.

"See." Seth waved an enthusiastic hand through the air. "The same arrogant Clint still lives. No skin off your back."

Laughing, they hopped into the truck, both already making notations on camera locations and where they needed to place some next.

~

She'd admit to avoiding Clint's various texts and phone calls. Bailey wasn't used to a man pursuing her, much less one that could sweet talk like Clint Hastings. All his messages began with *'Hey Beautiful,'* or *'Hey Firecracker.'* Cute, yes, but also nerve-racking. She wasn't sure if they were genuine or just careless flirting. With Clint it was hard to tell. They had an amazing time dove hunting and hanging out at Lawrence's. In fact, she didn't leave the ranch until almost midnight, they'd all talked on the back patio so late. And it was fun. She'd enjoyed her time with Clint, and even felt a spark. She even kissed him and still felt the thrill of it a week later. She was interested, but the more she thought about him and their time together, the more she realized she *wasn't* so sure about him. He seemed genuine in his feelings, but she also knew he had a reputation as a flirt. *Was he just flirting with her? Was their time together just a bit of fun to him?* She didn't like the feeling in her gut about the answer to that question. Why would Clint Hastings, the fun, flirty, rule-bending, and handsome cowboy, fall for a serious, rule-enforcing Bailey? He wouldn't. And therein lay her dilemma. She just couldn't trust her feelings or his intentions at the moment, so it was best to back off.

She'd had an insane work schedule the past week, and all she could think of was a nice weekend off and to herself. But that wasn't to be the case. And not only that, but she would need to stop her avoidance of Clint, because he was the one person she'd need to help her out. If he would. At this point, she'd gone cold. She hadn't responded to his last several texts or calls and they stopped coming. She'd dropped him, which she didn't feel proud about, but still kept telling herself it was necessary. *But how could she just pick up the phone and call him now?*

She leaned her head back against her seat and stared out the front of her windshield. She'd been parked off the side of the road leading into Parks for the last half hour trying to figure out her next move. She knew the answer to her question. She just had to do it. She had to just make the call.

She was a professional. She knew how to draw upon local ranchers and hunters for help in these cases. And he was good. She'd seen that with his tracking of the elk on his property and Chandler's. And she'd seen his marksmanship when they hunted dove. She needed Clint for the job. Sighing, she grabbed her cell phone and dialed.

"Well, well, well, Warden, I'm glad to see you're safe and sound." Clint's voice filtered over her truck speakers and her heart resounded with an erratic uptick in pace.

"Hi, Clint. Yes, I'm good."

He didn't respond, only waited for her to continue.

"Listen, I need your help. I've got reports and camera footage of a mountain lion in the area and some goats have been attacked. I need someone to help me hunt it down. Would you be interested?"

She could hear another brother in the background softly whispering though she couldn't make out the words. Finally, Clint spoke. "Yeah, okay. Where?"

"Well, I'm almost to Parks now. I can swing by and pick you up in about a half hour. We'll be heading over near Sanderson."

"That's fine. I'll be ready." He hung up.

He just... hung up. Just like that. No sweet talking, no nothing. Bailey rested her head against her steering wheel and took a couple of deep breaths before pulling out onto the highway and heading towards the 7H. What did she expect after ghosting him for a week after they'd shared a couple of intimate kisses? Her eyes stung, and she berated herself for the emotional embarrassment and frustration she felt coming over her. She'd screwed up, and dread at seeing him in person filled her stomach.

Forty minutes wasn't long enough to shake her out of her nerves. When she pulled to a stop in front of Clint's house and saw him walk out carrying a rifle, binoculars, and a box of ammo, her heart squeezed. He was so tall, she mused. Long legged, broad shouldered, defined jaw; everything a girl imagined when thinking of dreamy cowboys or handsome heroes. And she had been a jerk.

He opened her passenger door and climbed in, his knees almost hitting the dashboard in front of him. "Warden," he greeted, removing his cowboy hat and resting it on top of the dash in front of him. He situated his gun and supplies behind the seat and twisted back to the front, buckling his seatbelt as she reversed and headed back to the main entrance of the ranch. "A mountain lion, huh?"

She pointed to a file folder on her center console and watched as he flipped it open and studied the few pictures she'd received from a couple of ranchers. He gave a low whistle. "Good sized fella. I imagine a couple goats isn't all he's been feasting on."

"Try twenty-eight in two nights," Bailey reported.

"Ouch."

"Yeah. Definitely a problem. That could easily put a rancher out of the goat business."

"They try trappin' it?"

"Yes. This has been going on for a few weeks. This isn't the first property he's hit. He's crafty. Their concern is that his tracks have him moving towards a neighboring ranch that has cattle."

"Yeah, that won't go well."

"Exactly." She peered at him from the corner of her eye and liked how his eyes intensified when studying the photos. "You up for it?"

He glanced up, his blue eyes dancing. "For hunting? Always." He slipped the photos back into the folder and put it back in its spot. "I'm surprised you called me."

And here it was, she thought, the awkward confrontation. The one she deserved.

"Wasn't sure if you got lost or just ran away." He avoided her gaze and stared out the passenger window.

"Yeah, sorry about that. I was... thinking."

"That's always a good sign." Clint's voice held a touch of sarcasm. "I tend to lose them when they start thinking."

"Clint—"

"Look, don't worry about it." He held a hand up. "I get it. You don't have to explain. This ain't my first rodeo. Let's just focus on the mountain lion."

"You have your hunting license with you?"

He smirked. "Of course."

"Good. Though mountain lions are considered a 'non-game species', you still need a license to kill it."

He fished in his back pocket and fished out his license. "No handcuffs needed, Warden." He stuffed it back inside and shifted to slip it back into his pocket. "I'm fully legal to help you today."

"Good. And thanks. You were the first person I thought of when the other wardens and I were trying to map out a plan on bringing in outside help."

"I'm flattered." His voice told her he wasn't, but that he was trying to keep a friendly banter going. "You aren't taking me over to Chandler's place, are you? Because he'd be the only landowner I know that would refuse your 'outside help' once he found out it was me."

"No, not Chandler's. But why is that, anyway?"

"Well, it's not me personally," Clint pointed out. "I've never actually met the man in person before. Graham's the one usually dealing with him if there's a need. But the man hates us because we're Hastings. He and my granddaddy and daddy were always at each other's throats over property lines, fence repairs, snaring, oil. You name it, they fought about it. His prejudice did not die alongside them."

"That's sad."

Clint shrugged. "It is what it is. I tried calling him a few months ago about the elk tracks I was finding, but he wouldn't even let me get a word out."

"I know. I was there."

He turned to her in surprise. "What?"

"I was at Chandler's place when you called. I was meeting them, seeing their place."

"Well, that's somethin'. Yeah, he didn't like me callin' him. I thought the excitement of elk being on his property would be something we could partner with each other about, but he denied their presence. I know he was lying, though."

Her lack of response made him smirk. "You knew he was lying to me too."

"I did. His granddaughter was not pleased with the way he handled that situation, by the way. In fact, I think if you guys ever want to mend the bridge between the two ranches, she'd be your best bet. The next generation seems to be a little more open-minded."

"Doubt it. Chandlers and Hastings are like oil and water. They aren't ever going to mix."

"I hope that's not the case, because she's going to have her work cut out for her. A little neighborly support might be what she needs."

"I'll support her," Clint stated. "From afar."

Bailey turned onto a small dirt road that led into thick, heavy brush, the thorns and thistles scratching at her truck as she slowly made her way over deep ruts. "Going to set up in a stand."

"Alright."

"This one seemed most likely to be the next location he'd venture. We've got a couple of cameras set up. If I've timed it right, based on the camera footage, we have about an hour or so before he'll come hunting."

"I do love when a woman does her research." Clint hopped out of the truck and quietly shut the door. For a big man, he was light-footed, and Bailey didn't have to shush him once on their way to the stand. She reminded herself that Clint had been hunting since he was a little boy, and that he wasn't a newbie. He knew what he was doing. It's why she'd asked him to help her in the first place, but she respected his professionalism and focus on the task at hand. She could tell she'd upset him this week, but he was nudging aside those feelings to handle what they'd come to do. She climbed the ladder up into the stand and he followed, the small, cramped space even tighter with a man the size of Clint inside. They each had an old office chair to sit in that had both seen better days, but they were comfortable and allowed them to swivel quietly from window to window.

Clint set his gun in the corner, removing two bullets from his ammo box and slipping them into his shirt pocket.

Bailey could smell the light scent of him drift through the air at his movements, and her pulse drummed. His binoculars slipped from his lap to the floor with a thud, and they both leaned down to pick them up, their heads butting. She hissed, he grunted, and their eyes connected mere inches from one another. Neither moved. They just lingered in that awkward half-leaning, half-rising pose waiting on the other person to make a move or flee. She wasn't going to be the one. She'd made up her mind. She didn't want to lead him on anymore, but she also, stubbornly, didn't want to be the one to back away first. She wanted him to know she could handle being in tight spots with him. That they could be friends and move past the feelings they'd both begun to feel.

His fingers brushed hers as he slipped the binocs from her hand and her breath audibly caught at the contact, which caused a light spark to flare in his eyes. "Bailey," he whispered. "What is goin' on?" Nervous, she blinked and started to pull away, but his hand gently cupped her cheek and held her in place. "Talk to me."

"Now is not the time. We're here for work."

"We have an hour. You said so yourself. It's best to clear the air now, because I can't handle sittin' in here with you if it's going to be like this all evening." Clint removed his hand from her face and sat up, resting his binoculars in his lap.

"I just... I started thinking that it probably wasn't the best idea if we got involved with one another."

"Why's that?"

"Well—" She paused, realizing that her excuses and reasons didn't seem all that fair or important, and she didn't want to hurt his feelings. "Well, reasons."

"Reasons?" Clint's brow lifted and he huffed an annoyed breath. "Right."

"I'm not trying to be mean. I just— look, I just don't want to complicate things. My work is important to me."

"What does that even have to do with anything?" Clint asked. "I'm not coming after you and your job. I'm wanting to get to know you. Maybe even kiss you a little bit. Go on a few dates. See if we're something worth pursuing. I thought that was pretty clear last weekend. I also thought you were on board with that idea as well. If not, let's get it cleared up right now. I won't be mad, I just need to know. Because I don't like wastin' my time."

"You won't be mad?" she asked. "So it's not even that important to you?"

He sighed and ran a hand through his short hair. "Bailey, I'm not saying you're not important or that our relationship would not be important. I'm saying I won't hold a grudge. I'll be disappointed, maybe even a little irritated that it didn't go anywhere, but I won't stew about it."

"And you'll just move right along then, huh?" Her temper started to rise at the thought of him just being able to toss aside relationships so easily.

He shook his head. "You're not understanding me, or you're not trying to. I'm not trying to say I'll toss you aside and then go off with another pretty face the next day. That's not how I work, despite what some people might say or think."

"That's kind of what I've heard."

"Ah, so there it is." Clint snapped his fingers. "The real reason. You heard some 'bad boy Clint Hastings' stories and are running scared."

"I'm not scared," Bailey corrected.

"Right. Well, I have the answer I need, so we can just go back to watchin' for that lion now." Clint's jaw ticked as if he was biting back even more words to say, but his eyes focused ahead.

"Clint—"

"Shhh." He cut her off as he leaned forward, lifting his binoculars to his eyes. "Well, well, well. We got 'im." He handed her the binocs while he loaded his gun and lifted it into position. "I got him in sight."

"Range?" Bailey whispered.

"I need him to move out from behind that tree a bit more before I— got him." A shot rang out and Bailey watched as the mountain lion dropped to the ground. Thorough and quick. Both sat silent a moment. "Why did he have to kill the stinkin' goats?" Clint muttered.

"And four deer and two calves," Bailey added.

"You didn't tell me that."

"Well, on this particular ranch it's just been goats. But we've been trailing this guy for weeks. He was getting a little too close to the housing structures for comfort, and when bigger animals started dropping, then it became a problem."

"Yeah, I hate doing this. They're beauties. They're crafty, and the epitome of an efficient hunter, unlike canine predators like coyotes and wolves. It's amazing, really. Even though there's more mountain lions in the trans-Pecos area than anywhere else in the state combined, you rarely ever see them. Secretive, skilled, and elusive." Clint shook his head in disappointment. "But when a rancher's livelihood is at stake, he's got to go."

"Yeah, that was our worry too. Too many families rely on the land and their animals for him to let loose and have a feeding frenzy or train cubs to do the same."

Clint stood and climbed down the ladder. "You grab my gun, I'll get him."

She watched as he knelt beside the large animal and rubbed his hands over its fur. He lifted its large paws and took measurements. He knew she'd need those for record keeping and she appreciated his thoroughness. He then lifted it onto his back and across his shoulders. "Can I keep him? He's gorgeous. I'd like to see him at least become a beautiful mount."

"We'll have to fill out some paperwork, but I don't think it will be a problem."

Clint was gloomy the rest of the drive towards the 7H. She was a bit too at seeing such a creature have to be eliminated. But they'd also protected animals and people from its destructive path and that was something to be thankful for.

"Just drop me by the cooler and I'll put him in there for now."

She did as he asked, and Clint disappeared inside and came back out, washing his hands at the water hose on the side of the shed.

"Thanks for helping." Bailey climbed out of the truck and rounded the front. "Didn't take as long as I thought it would. I honestly thought we'd be scouting for a few days."

Clint shook his head. "Seems like you tracked him just fine on your own and just needed me to shoot... since I do have the better aim." He grinned and she rolled her eyes.

"Right. Well, thanks again anyway for being willing, you know, after... well, you know."

"No, I don't." He smiled, wanting her to continue fumbling over words. She shoved his shoulder and he laughed. "For real though, Bailey, I want to know why you went cold? Did you hear something about me? Did I offend you? Did I move too fast? I honestly want to know." His face sobered.

He never called her Bailey. It was always Warden. She liked the way he said her name, the long "A" sound dragged out for its own syllable. "I panicked."

"I see." He nodded in understanding. "I get that. I did too a little bit. Just ask Seth." He chuckled.

"You did?"

"Sure did. Well, I wouldn't say I panicked, per se. I just didn't really know what to make of you, is all. I mean, I've never had a woman just drop me like you did, especially after having such a good time with one another. It stung."

"Yeah, sorry about that." She wound her hands and he reached for them, brushing his thumbs over the tops of her knuckles. He tugged her towards him, and she willingly stepped forward.

"How about we just forget about runnin' scared from one another?" He bent down to meet her gaze until she looked up at him. "Because I'm not one to do that, and quite frankly, I don't believe you are either. You're one of the bravest women I've met in a long time, and that's sayin' something, because Julia married Graham and I didn't think I'd ever meet another woman as brave as her."

A soft laugh escaped her lips as he joked about his older brother.

"But I'm serious, Bailey. I want... well, I want you, if that's alright. And if I screw up, which I'm telling you now, I totally will because I do all the time, show me some grace, will ya? Because I want this. I want to try this out. I've never met a woman like you."

"Clint—"

"I'm not done," he interrupted. "You're smart, beautiful, stubborn, funny. A little irritating at times, but I'm willing to deal with that." His lips twitched into a quick grin before he continued. "As long as you're willing to do the same. So, what do you say? Will you let me woo you, Warden Keller?"

Her eyes flashed over his shoulder and her cheeks flushed as their audience, unbeknownst to Clint, all watched and waited for her reply. "I think it's worth a shot."

He cheered. "It will be." He kissed her solidly on the lips and started to deepen the kiss until he heard claps and whistles from a few people behind them. He pulled away quickly and then laughed as Lawrence walked up and slapped him on the back.

"Glad she said yes, or this would have been *real* awkward." Lawrence grinned as Calvin, Graham, and Seth stood a stone's throw away with the same chummy expressions.

"Me too." Clint held a hand to his heart. "But if she didn't, I'd have just cuffed our hands together until she warmed up to me."

Laughing, Bailey tugged his face to hers and kissed him. "No cuffs necessary, Hastings. No cuffs necessary.

Two Months Later

"Pass those potatoes, Lawrence." Annie held out her hand and scooped a helping onto Henry's plate. "Bailey, we're so glad you were able to finally join us." Annie passed the bowl to her and watched with approval as she took a hearty helping.

"And thank you, Clint, for the venison cutlets." Henry rubbed his stomach. "I sure do love when Annie fries them up so pretty."

"You're welcome. And there's more where that came from. We had a great season."

"That you did," Graham agreed, Clint surprised at the praise from his oldest brother.

"And now you know what to do for next year." Annie beamed at him.

"Oh, I have big plans for next season."

"Expansion," Seth pitched. "Maybe. If we could get some neighboring ranches on board."

"If you mean Chandler, forget about it." Calvin shook his head. "That ol' man won't have anything to do with us."

"I'm holding onto hope." Clint reached over and squeezed Bailey's hand. "And the good word from a respected warden. Besides, when they find out about the meat donation program, maybe they'll want to be a part of it. We gave away about 400 pounds this year. If we had more ranches on board for next year, we could double or triple that. Think of all the families that would benefit from that."

Julia walked up and placed a fresh bowl of salad on the table, lingering behind Clint and wrapping her arms around his neck for a brief hug. "We're all proud of you. You had a vision and you went for it. And Seth, you too." She gave the youngest brother a hug as well.

"And Graham's happy you stayed within budget," Philip quipped, Helena lightly slapping his thigh as he laughed.

"That I am." Graham gave an affirmative nod. "He had to proven the operation was viable. He did."

Clint leaned back in his chair and grinned. "You doubted me."

"Yep." Unashamed, Graham shrugged. "But I also don't mind being proved wrong." All the brothers laughed at that comment and Julia laid a comforting hand on her husband's arm with a small smile of her own.

"Hay," Ava's voice brought the brother's attention down to her. "You didn't get any of my potatoes."

Hayes waved for his brother to pass the bowl his way. He scooped a spoonful onto his plate.

"Those potatoes," began Annie. "are a picture no artist could make, Ms. Ava. A job well done."

Ava smiled proudly at Hayes as he took a quick bite. He made the appeasing sounds of approval and she turned excitedly towards Ally.

"Lawrence," Annie handed him a dish. "You want some caramelized onions, sweetie? I know you like 'em on your gravy." Annie wriggled the small tea plate in her hands, only one helping of onions on there meant for Lawrence.

"Oh, yes ma'am. They twang my buds, Annie. Thank you." He dumped them all on top of his plate.

"Spoiled rotten," Alice muttered. "Ruby's not going to know what to do with you."

"She's doing just fine." Lawrence grinned. "And loving me every minute of the day."

Alice rolled her eyes. "I bet." Calvin reached over and threaded his fingers through her ponytail, lightly kissing her cheek and pointing up the table for her to pass him one of the serving bowls.

"Al, you've been in a mood all week," Seth quipped. "What's up with that?"

"I haven't been in a mood," Alice defended. "I'm my normal charming self."

He scoffed. "Yeah, 'bout as bitter as burnt coffee most days."

Alice, taken aback, leaned against her chair. "That so?" She looked to Calvin for affirmation, and he avoided her eyes. "I see. Well, I'm not meaning to be. I'm just a little stressed at work trying to figure out what I'm going to do in several months when Julia's on maternity leave."

Julia gasped and Alice's eyes widened at letting the secret slip.

Philip and Hayes both choked on their drinks as Calvin's face split into a wide smile and he laughed. "I guess congratulations are in order." He reached over and shook Graham's hand.

"I'm sorry." Alice covered her mouth with her hands.

Annie jumped to her feet in a squeal as she rounded the table to hug Julia and Graham. "I can't believe it. I can't believe it! Henry, we're going to have a baby!"

Alice mouthed 'sorry' one more time to Julia, and her friend gave a simple wave signaling not to worry about it.

Clint reached over and gave a hearty slap to Graham's back before leaning over to Bailey. "I don't think Graham's come to terms with it yet."

"Why do you say that?" Bailey whispered, eyeing his oldest brother.

"Look how pale he is." Clint smirked and Bailey softly giggled.

"Poor guy. He won't know what hit him if it's a little girl."

Clint's eyes brightened with mischief. He raised his glass and stood. "A toast to the soon-to-be parents. Congrats, Graham and Jewels." Everyone clinked cups and glasses, little Ava excitedly bouncing in her seat to be included, her glass sloshing as she tapped it with a little more force than necessary against Hayes'. "So, what are you going to name her?"

"Her?!" Annie's eyes sparkled even more, and everyone started quizzing Graham and Julia about the baby. Not even listening for a confirmation of his assumption, Clint laughed.

"You love to stir the pot, don't you?" Bailey asked.

"Now, Warden, I'm offended." Grinning, he kissed her. "Guess you'll have to get used to it."

Kissing him again, she whispered, "I guess I will."

Continue the story with

https://www.amazon.com/dp/B099PZBKPD

INTRODUCING THE FAMILY
O'Rifcan
THE SIBLINGS O'RIFCAN SERIES
KH KATHARINE E. HAMILTON

The Complete Siblings O'Rifcan Series Available in Paperback, Ebook, and Audiobook

Claron
https://www.amazon.com/dp/B07FYR44KX

Riley
https://www.amazon.com/dp/B07G2RBD8D

Layla
https://www.amazon.com/dp/B07HJRL67M

Chloe
https://www.amazon.com/dp/B07KB3HG6B

Murphy
https://www.amazon.com/dp/B07N4FCY8V

All titles in The Lighthearted Collection Available in Paperback, Ebook, and Audiobook

Chicago's Best

https://www.amazon.com/dp/B06XH7Y3MF

Montgomery House

https://www.amazon.com/dp/B073T1SVCN

Beautiful Fury

https://www.amazon.com/dp/B07B527N57

McCarthy Road

https://www.amazon.com/dp/B08NF5HYJG

Check out the Epic Fantasy Adventure Available in Paperback, Ebook, and Audiobook

U~THE~NFADING LANDS

The Unfading Lands
https://www.amazon.com/dp/B00VKWKPES

Darkness Divided, Part Two in The Unfading Lands Series
https://www.amazon.com/dp/B015QFTAXG

Redemption Rising, Part Three in The Unfading Lands Series
https://www.amazon.com/dp/B01G5NYSEO

Subscribe to Katharine's Newsletter for news on upcoming releases and events!
https://www.katharinehamilton.com/subscribe.html

Find out more about Katharine and her works at:
www.katharinehamilton.com

Social Media is a great way to connect with Katharine. Check her out on the following:

Facebook: Katharine E. Hamilton
https://www.facebook.com/Katharine-E-Hamilton-282475125097433/

Twitter: @AuthorKatharine
Instagram: @AuthorKatharine

Contact Katharine:
khamiltonauthor@gmail.com

ABOUT THE AUTHOR

Katharine E. Hamilton began writing in 2008 and published her first children's book, The Adventurous Life of Laura Bell in 2009. She would go on to write and illustrate two more children's books, Susie At Your Service and Sissy and Kat between 2010-2013.

Though writing for children was fun, Katharine moved into Adult Fiction in 2015 with her release of The Unfading Lands, a clean, epic fantasy that landed in Amazon's Hot 100 New Releases on its fourth day of publication, reached #72 in the Top 100 in Epic Fantasy, and hit the Top 10,000 Best Sellers on all of Amazon in its first week. It has been listed as a Top 100 Indie Read for 2015 and a nominee for a Best Indie Book Award for 2016. The series did not stop there. Darkness Divided: Part Two of The Unfading Land Series, released in October of 2015 and claimed a spot in the Top 100 of its genre. Redemption Rising: Part Three of The Unfading Lands Series released in April 2016 and claimed a nomination for the Summer Indie Book Awards.

Though comfortable in the fantasy genre, Katharine decided to venture towards romance in 2017 and released the first novel in a collection of sweet, clean and wholesome romances: The Lighthearted Collection. Chicago's Best reached best seller status in its first week of publication and rested comfortably in the Top 100 for Amazon for three steady weeks, claimed a Reader's Choice Award, a TopShelf Indie Book Award, and ended up a finalist in the American Book Festival's

Best Book Awards for 2017. <u>Montgomery House</u>, the second in the collection, released in August of 2017 and rested comfortably alongside its predecessor, claiming a Reader's Choice Award, and becoming Katharine's best-selling novel up to that point. Both were released in audiobook format in late 2017 and early 2018. <u>Beautiful Fury</u> is the third novel released in the collection and has claimed a Reader's Choice Award and a gold medal in the Authorsdb Best Cover competition. It has also been released in audiobook format with narrator Chelsea Carpenter lending her talents to bring it to life. Katharine and Chelsea have partnered on an ongoing project for creating audiobook marketing methods for fellow authors and narrators, all of which will eventually be published as a resource tool for others.

In August of 2018, Katharine brought to life a new clean contemporary romance series of a loving family based in Ireland. The Siblings O'Rifcan Series kicked off in August with <u>Claron</u>. <u>Claron</u> climbed to the Top 1000 of the entire Amazon store and has reached the Top 100 of the Clean and Wholesome genre a total of 11 times. He is Katharine's bestselling book thus far and lends to the success of the following books in the series: <u>Riley</u>, <u>Layla</u>, <u>Chloe</u>, and <u>Murphy,</u> each book earning their place in the Top 100 of their genre and Hot 100 New Releases. <u>Claron</u> was featured in Amazon's Prime Reading program March – June 2019. The series is also available in audiobook format with the voice talents of Alex Black.

A Love For All Seasons, a Sweet Contemporary Romance Series launched in July of 2019 with

Summer's Catch, followed by Autumn's Fall in October. Winter's Call and Spring's Hope scheduled for 2021 release dates. The series follows a wonderful group of friends from Friday Harbor, Washington, and has been Katharine's newest and latest project.

Katharine has contributed to charitable Indie Anthologies as well as helped other aspiring writers journey their way through the publication process. She manages an online training course that walks fellow self-publishing and independently publishing writers through the publishing process as well as how to market their books.

She is a member of Women Fiction Writers of America, Texas Authors, IASD, and the American Christian Fiction Writers. She loves everything to do with writing and loves that she is able to continue sharing heartwarming stories to a wide array of readers.

Katharine graduated from Texas A&M University with a bachelor's degree in History. She lives on a ranch in south Texas with her husband Brad, sons Everett, and West, and their two dogs, Tulip and Paws.

Printed in Great Britain
by Amazon